JENNI

More Jennings books to watch out for:

1 JENNINGS GOES TO SCHOOL
2 THANKS TO JENNINGS
3 ESPECIALLY JENNINGS
4 JENNINGS IN PARTICULAR
5 SPEAKING OF JENNINGS
6 TRUST JENNINGS
7 TYPICALLY JENNINGS
8 THE JENNINGS REPORT

and the brand-new Jennings book
JENNINGS AGAIN!

Author's note

Each of the Jennings books is a story complete in itself. Apart from the first title, JENNINGS GOES TO SCHOOL, the books can be read in any order, and for this reason I have chosen some of the later titles for early publication in this edition.

Anthony Buckeridge

JENNINGS, OF COURSE!

Anthony Buckeridge

for John and Andrew Williams

First published 1964 by William Collins & Sons Co Ltd

Paperback edition with illustrations by Rodney Sutton, published 1991 by MACMILLAN CHILDREN'S BOOKS
A division of Pan Macmillan Children's Books Limited
London and Basingstoke
Associated companies throughout the world

ISBN 0-333-55660-7

A CIP catalogue record for this book is available from the British Library

Typeset by Macmillan Production Limited
Printed in Great Britain by Richard Clay Ltd, Bungay, Suffolk

CONTENTS

LIST OF ILLUSTRATIONS

Chapter 1

Wrong Foot Foremost

The bell rang for the end of morning school. In Form Three classroom, Mr Wilkins swung round from the blackboard and tossed the chalk on to the master's desk.

"Right! Stop working and put your things away," he ordered. "In silence, mind. No noise; no talking!"

Books closed with a clap, desk lids shot open sending pens and rulers slithering to the floor, while from all over the room arose the hum, gargle and buzz of boys exercising their lungs without actually speaking; the hiss of imaginary air-brakes mingled with the whine of space-rockets leaving imaginary launching pads. It was as though the seventeen boys of Form Three having rested their voices for the past forty minutes, were now tuning up their vocal machinery for a mechanical concert.

"Quietly, I said . . . *Quietly*!" Mr Wilkins' booming voice drowned the orchestra. "I shan't dismiss this class until everyone's stopped fidgeting, and it's so silent you could hear a pin drop."

The noise died away. Engines were throttled back,

bombs ceased exploding and the space-rockets went into soundless orbit. Eager for their release the class sat stockstill with folded arms, resisting the urge to wriggle.

With one exception! In the back row a hand was flapping like a duster on a washing-line to attract the master's attention.

Mr Wilkins frowned at the flapping hand. He, too, was anxious to be on his way. "What's the matter, Jennings?" he demanded.

"Well, sir, it's about this pin you're going to drop," the boy replied. "Have you actually got one on you? Because if not, I could easily go up to Matron's room and ask her if she'd very kindly lend . . . "

"You'll do nothing of the sort," snapped Mr Wilkins. "I'm waiting to dismiss the class, so don't waste time asking silly questions."

"Sorry, sir," Jennings apologised, but the idea of a pin-dropping ceremony intrigued him and a further query sprang to his mind. "The only thing is, sir, that some blokes might be a bit deafer than others, and if they were sitting at the back they might not hear it. So don't you think it would be a good idea if all the blokes who thought they might be a bit deaf were to sit in the front row and . . . "

"Silence!" thundered Mr Wilkins at the top of his powerful voice. He was a large man with a brusque manner and a limited supply of patience. Though genuinely fond of the boys in his care he could never quite understand the workings of the eleven-year-old mind. The things boys said and the things boys did seemed fantastic to a grown-up of his way of thinking.

Here was a case in point! If those silly little boys imagined he was going to carry out hearing tests to discover who could hear a pin drop, and who couldn't! . . . The idea was preposterous! Besides, he hadn't *got* a pin. His threat had been a mere figure of speech which anyone with his head screwed on the right way would have understood at once.

But not Jennings, of course! In the opinion of L. P. Wilkins, Esq, MA, Jennings' head was screwed on so precariously that the slightest breath of commonsense set it wobbling on his shoulders like a jelly on a fast-moving dinner-trolley.

"Nobody will leave this room until there has been absolute silence for the space of thirty seconds," the master went on in ominous tones. "If I hear the slightest sound during that time, I shall—I shall—well, there'd better not *be* any sound." He glanced at his watch. "Thirty seconds, starting from now."

Form Three classroom was a tomb of silence. Each boy was tense with the strain of not moving, not blinking, not breathing.

Twenty-seven seconds ticked away. Satisfied, Mr Wilkins opened his mouth to dismiss the class. As he did so, a table-tennis ball slipped from its owner's clumsy fingers and bounced once, twice, three times on the echoing floorboards. In the stillness of the room the sound punctured the silence like pistol shots.

Mr Wilkins was furious. "I—I—I—Who dropped that thing?" he barked.

The hand in the back row was raised again. "I did, sir, but I didn't mean to. It was an accident, honestly. I was just holding it and it slipped . . . "

"Jennings, of course! It *would* be," fumed Mr Wilkins, as the ball having finished its resonant bouncing rolled along the aisle between the desks.

As it reached the front row, Venables, an untidy twelve-year-old, put out his foot to stop it. Misjudging the force required for so delicate a manoeuvre, he placed his foot down too heavily. There was a *plop*, and the ball lay squashed beneath his thick-soled shoe.

Jennings was furious! "Oh, sir, look what Venables has done, sir!" he protested.

Mr Wilkins was in no mood to offer sympathy. "Serves you right for playing with it at the wrong time."

"I wasn't playing with it, sir. I was just holding it ready till you said we could go," Jennings defended himself. "Besides, it's not even my ball, sir – it's yours."

"Mine?" Mr Wilkins was surprised. Table-tennis was a game he seldom played. And then he remembered lending the boy an unclaimed ball which had been handed in as lost property months before. Mr Wilkins certainly didn't want it back: there was far too much clutter in the lost property cupboard as it was. On the other hand, a borrower must learn to fulfil his obligations. "In that case you'll have to buy me another one, won't you!" he said.

When the class had been dismissed and Mr Wilkins' heavy footfall had died away along the corridor, Jennings rounded on Venables with some heat.

"You clumsy great troll, plonking your outsize elephant's hoof on it like a sabre-toothed pile-driver," he complained. "Ping-pong balls aren't cannon balls, you know."

"Sorry," the culprit grinned. "All the same, I don't see that you've got much to moan about. If it hadn't busted, Old Wilkie would have confiscated it, so you'd have lost it anyway."

Atkinson, Temple, Bromwich and other third-formers gathered round and joined in the debate, shouting into one another's ears in tones suggesting that the group were all in need of hearing-aids. The balance of opinion was in Venables' favour, and most of the arguers held that Jennings had only himself to blame for his misfortunes.

Only Darbishire remained loyal to his friend. "It's all right, Jen," he confided when the crowd had dispersed. "I've got an old ping-pong ball you can have for Sir. It's a bit bent because of that time we played hockey with it behind the boot-lockers, but I sucked the dents out and I don't suppose he'll mind if it doesn't bounce all that well."

"Thanks, Darbi. Really great of you," Jennings replied.

"Mind you, I *would* like just one last game with it before it disappears into Sir's clutches. How about you and me having a famous international ping-pong tournament after lunch?"

Jennings glanced out of the window at the rain teeming down on the playing-field. It would certainly be too wet for football that afternoon.

"Righto, then. Just you and me, eh? And the winner will be Champion of the World and Outer Space!"

They turned towards each other with right arms extended and pressed their thumbs together. The gesture was a sign that a pact had been agreed. Let no-one break a bond solemnly sealed by the pressure of two ink-stained thumbs!

There was a comfortable, easy-going friendship between Jennings and Darbishire, though each was as different from the other as rhyme from reason. Jennings was the taller of the two, and had about him the eager air of one who acts first and thinks afterwards. Though full of good intentions, his well-sprung plans were apt to recoil and his shafts of inspiration to fall wide of their target.

His friend Darbishire was of a more cautious disposition. Fair-haired and curly with mild blue eyes behind his ink-splashed glasses, he was a staunch follower but never a leader in the exploits and misadventures of boarding-school life. As Jennings' right-hand man he often found himself an unwilling partner in situations which he viewed with alarm.

The lunch bell rang, and the two contenders for the *Ping-Pong Championship of Outer Space* hurried off to the dining-hall to fortify themselves for the contest with lukewarm fish pie and stewed rhubarb.

Unlike football and cricket, table-tennis did not depend upon the season for its following. The table in the games room was always available, yet the popularity of the game waxed and waned for no apparent reason.

For some time past interest had been at a low ebb, so Jennings and Darbishire were surprised to hear the *ping* and *pong* of bat on ball as they approached the games room after the rest period following the midday meal. Inside, they found Venables and Atkinson patting the ball across the net with great energy and little skill.

"Tut! They've beaten us to it," Jennings grumbled. "That's your fault, Darbi. If only you hadn't wasted time putting your gym shoes on, we'd have been here first."

"I *had* to change," Darbishire argued. "You can't compete in famous Outer Space tournaments wearing heavy great clodhoppers like diver's boots. You've got to be on your toes, darting about like a streak of lightning."

Jennings snorted. "Streak of lightning! Huh! Fifty million gym shoes wouldn't help *you* get the ball over the net. Honestly, Darbi, your ping-pong's chronic! All you do is prance about like a carthorse with chilblains and miss the ball whenever it comes near you." Impatiently, he turned to the table-tennis players. "How much longer are you two going to be? We've got an important match to play."

"We'll be hours yet," said Venables. "Atki keeps forgetting the score, so we have to go back to the beginning again."

The spectators perched themselves on the radiator and waited and watched. It was clear that Venables was the better player, and gradually the score rose to twenty points to nine in his favour. Then, with only one point needed for victory, he started playing with wanton carelessness and lost seven points in succession.

"Hey, that's not fair," Jennings complained. "You're losing on purpose just to make it last longer."

"No, I'm not," grinned Venables. "It's you watching me. Your face is putting me off my stroke." He turned to his opponent. "What's the score now, Atki?"

"Twenty – sixteen."

"Well, in that case we ought to have changed service before the last point. Better go back and play it again, eh?"

"No flipping fear," Jennings protested. "That's just a trick to keep Darbi and me off the table."

The protest was ignored. Atkinson flourished his bat, called out "Service!" – and hit the ball into the net.

Jennings was delighted. "Game to Venables! Twenty-one – sixteen!" he crowed. "Come on Darbi! Now for ye famous challenge match."

The winner glowered at his opponent. "What did you want to lose that point for! If you'd just patted it, we could have kept going for hours."

The newcomers took their places at the table, but even before the ball was in play a bell rang in the hall below. Almost immediately Mr Carter, the senior master, appeared in the doorway.

"Go and get your outdoor clothes," he told them. "It's stopped raining now and Mr Wilkins is taking you for a walk."

The announcement was received with muffled groans. "Oh, sir, not a *walk*, sir!" Jennings pleaded. "Darbishire and I have been waiting hours to bag the table, and now we've got to stop before we've even started."

"Too bad!" Mr Carter sympathised. "You'll have to postpone your game till you get back, that's all." His tone was friendly, his smile was reassuring.

The boys liked Mr Carter, for he could be relied

upon to look at things from their point of view – even though he might not always agree with it. He knew a great deal about what went on in the developing minds of the boys whom he taught and – unlike Mr Wilkins – he treated them as fully-grown members of their own age group.

As the four boys made their way downstairs Atkinson said, "You needn't think you can have first go on the table when we get back, Jennings. You can't bag it in advance, you know."

"But we haven't had our turn yet. We never even got started."

"That's your bad luck. When we get home from the walk again, it'll be first come first served."

"That's right," Venables agreed. "Tell you what! We'll walk together, Atki, you and me and—" He cupped his hands round his mouth and whispered the rest of his plan into his friend's ear.

Atkinson grinned as he listened to the secret plan, and was still grinning as he and Venables pranced away together to fetch their caps and coats.

Darbishire scowled after the prancing conspirators. "Anyone can see what they're planning to do," he said scathingly. "Serves them right if Old Wilkie catches them. He probably will, too. We came unstuck the last time we tried that old dodge."

Venables' plan was simple enough, and had been tried by most of the boys at one time or another. According to the school rule the boys were supposed to keep ahead of the master in charge of the walk, but it was sometimes possible to drop behind without being observed and to dawdle along slowly until the main body was well ahead. Thus, when the master blew his whistle as a signal to turn about, the walkers in the rear found themselves in the lead, and could hurry home with little risk of being overtaken.

The drawback to this scheme was that the staff knew all about it and would be quick to thwart the intentions of any laggard skulking at the back for no good reason. But there was always a chance that the master wouldn't notice!

"I've got a much better idea," Jennings decided as they took their outdoor clothes down from their pegs. "We'll do it the other way round, and get so far ahead of Sir that he can't see us."

"What's the good of that? We'd have even farther to walk back when the whistle blew," Darbishire objected.

"No, we shouldn't. As soon as we're out of sight, we'll take cover and hide till everyone else has gone past, including Venables and Atki."

"Yes, of course. Great idea!" Darbishire approved as the advantages of the scheme dawned upon him. "And then when *they're* out of sight, round a bend or somewhere, we can turn round and belt back like four-minute milers." He laughed aloud. "Poor old Ven and Atki! They won't half look a couple of Charleys when they come charging back and find us halfway through our game."

"That's what we'll do then! Secret pact!"

The pact was pledged by the ritual of pressing their thumbs together. Then they hurried outside on to the playground where Mr Wilkins was shepherding his flock for their afternoon's exercise.

"Now, all stand still and listen to me," the master ordered. "We're going over the meadow past Arrowsmith's farm as far as the village and back. There's to be no lagging behind on the way. Everyone's to keep well in front of me."

Jennings winked at Darbishire and said, "That's all right, sir. You won't have to wait for *us* to catch up, will he, Darbi?"

Darbishire glanced sharply at his friend. It was all very well to make private jokes on the assumption that Mr Wilkins wouldn't see the point, but it was risky all the same.

Mr Wilkins gave the order to start and the seventy-nine boarders of Linbury Court set off through the school gates and along the footpath towards the village.

Jennings and Darbishire scurried to the front and set a lively pace along the footpath. The rain had stopped and the sun was doing its best to pierce the lowering November clouds, but the ground was soggy, and puddles filled the ruts made by Mr Arrowsmith's tractors and trailers.

By the time they reached the gate leading to the second field the two boys were well ahead of Mr Wilkins' party. Here the path skirted a small wood and then veered off towards the left, so that once round the bend the boys were out of sight of their colleagues. They were still some distance from the entrance to Arrowsmith's farmyard and Jennings decided that they had reached an ideal spot for going into hiding.

"Now's our chance. Sir won't be coming over the

horizon for at least ten minutes," he said, leading the way to a gap in the hedge which bordered the footpath for a hundred yards in each direction.

"Phew! Thank goodness for that." Darbishire blew out his cheeks and mopped his brow. "The speed we came round that last corner, I nearly shot off into orbit."

The hedge was thick enough at that point to conceal their presence from anyone passing by on the footpath, so they squeezed through the gap and found themselves standing on top of a bank which sloped steeply down to a ditch at the bottom, some eight feet below. The surface was slippery and they had to move with care in order to preserve a foothold.

"Wow! It's pretty chronic around these parts!" Darbishire complained. "Every time you take a step it goes *ger-squilch, ger-squelch.*"

"Never mind that. The first thing to do is to get ourselves camouflaged before the others come along. Better kneel down to be on the safe side."

Nettles and thistles grew all over the bank, so they took off their raincoats and folded them into makeshift cushions to protect their knees. For some minutes they crouched in silence on their knee-pads. Then Darbishire said, "Supposing they're not coming! Supposing Old Wilkie's turned the walk round and they're all belting back home."

"Not yet, he wouldn't. Not till they've got to Arrowsmith's farm."

Still, it would do no harm to make sure, Jennings decided. He stood up and poked his head through the gap in the hedge to see whether the vanguard was in sight. A glimpse of crimson school caps in the distance reassured him.

"It's all right! They're just coming," he called out – and stepped backwards on to a slippery mud-patch running down to the ditch below.

For a split second his feet skated at all angles as he tried to regain his balance. Then, out of control, he slid down the bank like a kangaroo on a ski-jump and landed on all fours in the two-foot depth of mud and water at the bottom of the ditch.

Chapter 2

In Hazard

The splash sent a shower of ditch-water high into the air. A moment later, with mud sucking at his ankles and dripping from his elbows, Jennings heaved himself back on to the bank like a crocodile emerging from a swamp.

From head to foot he was plastered with the rich fertile silt of the waterlogged subsoil. Prostrate with shock, he knelt gasping on the bank while Darbishire, numb with horror and dismay, stared down at him from the shelter of the hedge.

"Oh, my goodness! Fossilised fish-hooks! Whatever happened?" he quavered.

Jennings didn't answer. Considering that Darbishire had been a witness to the accident the question seemed somewhat unnecessary. Besides, he was wet through, chilled to the bone, and his teeth were chattering so violently that for the moment speech was out of the question.

"Wow, I've never seen such a mess," Darbishire went on. "Look at your suit. Look at your socks! You remind me of that song about hippopotamuses wallowing in glorious mud."

"Never mind what song I remind you of. Help me up the bank before Sir gets here," Jennings retorted as the power of speech returned. "If he sees me like this, there'll be frantic hoo-hah."

"Yes, of course." Taking care not to lose his foothold, Darbishire edged forward and seized Jennings' mud-caked hand. What to do about the appalling state of his clothes was something they would have to consider later on. What mattered more at the moment was to conceal the facts of the disaster from Mr Wilkins.

With difficulty the boys scrambled back up the bank and crouched down once again in their hiding place.

They were only just in time. Voices raised in friendly argument came wafting through the hedge as the walkers in the lead approached along the footpath. Jennings and Darbishire could see them from the knees downwards through the gap between the foliage and the hedge-roots.

Temple, Bromwich and Rumbelow, easily identified by their voices, were striding along together well in advance of the main body of walkers.

"What's the point of choosing the best football team in the whole world if there's nobody good enough to play against them!" Temple was saying in ringing tones. "And it wouldn't be any use sending them to Mars, or somewhere. We don't even know if there are *people* on Mars, let alone whether they play football."

"I bet there are," replied Rumbelow. "Not ordinary human beings like you and me, of course, but special

Jennings and Darbishire could see them from the knees downwards.

little men with things like television aerials coming out of their heads and perhaps, say, for instance, eight arms and legs."

"You'd have a job teaching *them* to play football!" Bromwich said scathingly. "They'd need four pairs of boots each to begin with, and they'd puncture the ball every time they tried to head it."

The discussion on the Earth XI's chances of winning the football championship of the Solar System died away as the debaters moved out of earshot. After a short pause Martin-Jones and Thompson came along arguing about pop records, followed by Binns and Blotwell trying to decide whether school tea tasted more like diesel oil or cabbage water.

In groups of twos and threes the walkers straggled past, broadcasting opinions and snippets of information to the fugitives behind the hedge. Then Mr Wilkins' voice was heard close at hand and Jennings and Darbishire grew tense with anxiety.

There had always been a risk that their plan might fail. This would have been bad enough in any circumstances, but now, with the chief conspirator dyed a streaky black from eyebrows to ankles, discovery would spell disaster on a scale that set the imagination rocking on its pinions.

"Come along, you boys, double up there! . . . Venables! . . . Atkinson! I've already told you three times not to lag behind." Mr Wilkins' tone was brusque and Jennings felt consoled by the thought that the plans of the opposing faction had been frustrated.

"Yes, sir. Just coming, sir!" Wellington boots came into view in the space beneath the hedge, and stopped a moment later at the spot where Jennings and Darbishire had forced their way through. Then Venables' voice rang out again.

"Sir, please, sir, there's a gap here. May Atkinson and I go through and see where it leads to?"

Here was fresh cause for alarm! Even though Venables would not purposely betray their hiding place, any exclamation of surprise might well warn Mr Wilkins that something odd was going on behind the hedge.

But all was well, for the master said, "You'll do nothing of the sort. I'm not having you boys playing around in the mud. You'll be falling into the ditch before you know where you are."

The wellingtons passed out of sight and the voices drifted out of earshot as Mr Wilkins and his party resumed their walk.

Jennings was only too thankful to hear them go. The sun had disappeared and rain-clouds had been gathering for the past few minutes. He was cold, wet and miserable, but he knew it wouldn't be safe to leave their hiding place until Mr Wilkins was past the gateway to the farmyard.

Just then, he felt the first drop of rain on the back of his neck. He stood upright and said, "Wait there, Darbi, I'll go and see if they're nearly out of sight."

"Well, for goodness' sake be more careful this time," Darbishire advised. "If you start doing another of your famous nose-dives . . . " He broke off in alarm as the blast of a referee's whistle sounded from farther along the lane. "Oh, fish-hooks! Hear that, Jen! Sir's blowing the 'about turn' already. Oh, slithering snakes! Why did it have to start raining *now*!"

It was indeed the lowering clouds with their threat of more rain to come that had caused Mr Wilkins to change his plans and cut short the afternoon walk. For Jennings and Darbishire his decision could not have come at a worse moment.

Either they must leave their hide-out with Mr Wilkins dangerously close at hand, or remain concealed until the walkers had retraced their steps and disappeared from view in the opposite direction.

Darbishire was anxious to be gone. "Come on quick," he urged, seizing his raincoat and making for the gap.

Jennings grabbed his shoulder and forced him down on his knees again.

"It's too late. We haven't time," he pointed out. "They'll be back round the bend in two bats of an eyelid. Old Wilkie knows we weren't walking behind him, so if he sees us in front he'll know we weren't there before he turned round."

Darbishire looked blank. "Say that again. 'If he sees us in front he'll know we're not behind!' . . . "

"Oh, don't be so feeble," Jennings broke in irritably. "The point is we've perishing well got to stay here till they've all gone past."

"But what about the ping-pong? The whole idea of hiding was so's we could get home first."

"Yes, I know, but . . . "

"Honestly, Jen, you're the most shrimp-witted troll I've ever met," fumed Darbishire. "You and your famous ideas! What did you want to go and fall in for!"

"I didn't *want* to fall in," Jennings defended himself. "You don't think I go splashing into squelching wet ditches full of slimy black water in the middle of winter, just for my own selfish pleasure, do you!"

Again they heard the whistle, followed by Mr Wilkins' voice shouting to the stragglers to catch up. The voice sounded dangerously close.

Darbishire crouched on his raincoat. This was positively the last time he was going to have anything to do with Jennings' crackbrained ideas, he told himself. . . . Positively the last time!

By now the walkers were all trekking homewards. In the lead were Venables and Atkinson moving at a brisk trot with every prospect of laying first claim to the ping-pong table. Then, in reverse order, the groups of two's and three's passed by the gap in the hedge.

Bringing up the rear and flanking Mr Wilkins on both sides came Temple, Bromwich and Rumbelow, still selecting unlikely players for improbable football teams.

"How about Oliver Cromwell in goal, and William the Conqueror at centre half?" Temple was saying as he came into earshot.

"That's no good. William the Conqueror was a Norman so he wouldn't be qualified to play for an *All England History XI*," Bromwich objected. "You could have him for the *Rest of Europe* if you like."

"We've already got Julius Caesar as centre half for the *Rest*. I vote we put William the Conq. out on the left wing instead of Christopher Columbus."

Rumbelow turned to Mr Wilkins for advice. "Sir,

please, sir, if you were picking a football team from history, would you choose Henry the Eighth or Shakespeare for centre forward?"

"Don't talk such ridiculous nonsense," Mr Wilkins reproved. "And for goodness' sake walk faster. I want to get home before it comes on to rain any harder."

Their voices died away in the distance, but it was not until some minutes later that Jennings decided that it was safe to leave their hiding place.

"Old Wilkie's got eyes like a photostatic burglar alarm," he informed his long-suffering friend. "He's only got to look round and we'll be properly up the creek."

"Pity you didn't think of that before," Darbishire grumbled as he rose to his feet. "You and your famous ideas for getting home first!"

Keeping well in the shelter of the hedge they followed the walk at a safe distance until they came within sight of the school gates. Here they stopped to consider their next move. Fortunately Mr Wilkins hadn't noticed their absence, and much depended now upon whether Jennings could smuggle himself into the building and change his clothes without meeting a member of the staff. It was a lucky chance that he had taken off his raincoat before his ill-fated plunge, for now, at any rate, he was adequately covered from shoulders to knees.

No one was about as they crept in through the side door and made their stealthy way along the passage. Then Jennings went off to the wash-basins in the basement, while Darbishire climbed the stairs to Dormitory Four on the second floor. As he passed the open door of the games room he heard the *ping* and *pong* of bat on ball and squawks of happy, carefree laughter coming from within . . . Venables and Atkinson were clearly enjoying their game!

Darbishire snorted in disgust. It was all very well for *some* people to prance about laughing their silly heads off: *other* people didn't think the joke was funny at all.

School uniform in the winter months consisted of a shirt and shorts and a heavy sweater. The regulation colour was grey, brightened only by a red tie and a band of the same shade round sock-tops and sweater neck.

There was a spare sweater and shorts and several shirts and socks on Jennings' shelf in the cupboard in Dormitory Four. Darbishire chose the clothes his friend needed and hurried downstairs, keeping a sharp lookout for Matron on the way.

When he reached the changing room he found his friend clad in raincoat and underclothes, scowling at the sodden bundle of garments he had taken off and stacked on the radiator.

"It's hopeless trying to get this bunch cleaned up," Jennings grumbled as he put on his spare clothes. "I'm not worried about my socks – they could have got muddy on the playing field or anywhere. And my shirt isn't too bad because it was underneath. But just *look* at my trousers and sweater! What on earth's Matron going to say when she sees that lot!"

Darbishire gave a helpless shrug. Somehow the soiled clothes looked even more disreputable now that

Jennings had taken them off. The rich silt which was such a proud feature of Mr Arrowsmith's agricultural subsoil had dyed the garments in an irregular pattern of splodges and stripes. The removal of the stains was clearly a job for experts: unskilled efforts to remove them with carbolic soap and lukewarm water might well make matters worse.

"Matron will go through the roof if she finds these in the laundry basket," Jennings went on. "She'll want to know how it happened, and then it'll all come out about hiding from Sir on the walk and everything."

Matron was known for her willingness to lend a friendly ear to the troubles of the young. But this would be straining the bonds of friendship too far. Besides even if she *didn't* tell anyone, the truth might easily leak out. Masters had a flair for unearthing facts that they were not supposed to know.

"What are you going to do then – if you can't send them to the laundry?" Darbishire demanded.

Jennings thought for a while and then his face lit up with inspiration. "I'll take them to the cleaners in Dunhambury on Saturday afternoon," he said.

Darbishire was appalled at the boldness of the plan.

"What! Go in by bus *without permish*! You're bonkers! Besides, you wouldn't have time to get there and back without being missed."

In theory, Jennings' plan sounded reasonable enough. Saturday was a half-holiday, and as there was no football fixture arranged for that day the boys would be playing practice games, starting at a quarter to three. Lunch finished just before one-thirty, and the half-hourly bus to the market town of Dunhambury, some five miles away, was due outside the school gates at forty minutes past the hour.

It would, therefore, be possible to reach Dunhambury a few minutes before two o'clock, leave the clothes at the dry cleaners in the High Street and catch the two twenty-five bus back to Linbury, arriving on the football pitch just in time for the start of the game.

Darbishire was quick to put his finger on the more risky aspects of the plan.

"You won't have time to change for football after you get back," he pointed out.

"OK, then, I'll change before I go. Straight after lunch and put my raincoat on top, so when I get back I can go straight on to the pitch. Old Wilkie will think I've just come out of the changing room with the others."

"But what about getting your clothes back? What about paying for them? It'll probably cost a small fortune to get all that muck off."

Again Jennings had a ready answer. "I'll ask them to send the bill to my mother."

The plan had a ring of adventure about it with its hint of synchronised watches, split-second timing and furtive dashes to and from the bus stop. Darbishire tingled with excitement. It was the sort of plan that sent shivers of apprehension down his spine. He, personally, would never dream of attempting such a risky manoeuvre, but if old Jennings thought he could get away with it – well, good luck to him! In fact, he . . .

Darbishire's train of thought stopped with a jolt as he realised that Jennings was still explaining the details of his plan, and was talking about them in the first person plural.

"*We*! What do you mean '*we*'?" Darbishire echoed in horrified tones. "This is your idea, not mine. I'm not coming with you."

"Of course you are. It'll be much easier with two of us. I may need someone to run ahead and keep the bus waiting or I may need . . . "

"No thank you! If you want to go ahead with this crackbrained scheme that's your headache, but you can definitely include me out." Darbishire spoke with some heat. His whole nature rebelled at taking part in so perilous an enterprise.

"But we're in this together, Darbi," Jennings urged. "In fact, it was all your fault that I skidded into the ditch in the first place."

"My fault! Well, I like the cheek of that!"

"Of course it was! Who wanted a last game with his ping-pong ball? . . . You did! Who agreed it'd be a good idea to hide behind the hedge and get home first? . . . You did! . . . Who . . . "

"Oh, all right, all right!" Darbishire said peevishly. He knew from past experience that it was hopeless to argue with Jennings when once he had made up his mind. "I suppose I'll *have* to come if you're going to be pigheaded about it. But I don't like it. I don't like it one little bit."

The tea bell put an end to the argument. Jennings hid his dirty clothes in his tuck-box and together they made their way upstairs to line up outside the dining hall.

There was nothing more they could do about the

dry-cleaning operation until Saturday afternoon. And that was five days ahead. Meanwhile, it would be better to forget the hazards to come by devoting their leisure time to some less dangerous activity.

Chapter 3

Surprise Item

There was an hour's free time between the end of evening prep and the sounding of the dormitory bell.

Darbishire decided to do some painting. The afternoon's disaster had left him in no mood for table-tennis, and he wanted to find some quiet occupation to take his mind off the nerve-racking enterprise planned for the weekend.

His paint-box was not in his locker where it should have been. He frowned and, thinking back, remembered lending it to Jennings some three weeks before on the strict understanding that it was to be returned the following day.

Darbishire's frown deepened. The resentment he had felt earlier at being coerced against his will had been simmering throughout evening prep. Now it came to the boil and overflowed.

He turned and shouted across the room, "Hey, Jennings! You're a gruesome ruin and you've had your chips this time, so you'd flipping well better watch out!"

Jennings looked up from his library book in surprise.

"Wow! You sound mighty fierce, Darbi. What's up?"

"What's up!" Darbishire echoed. "It's what *isn't* up that I'm moaning about. Where's my paint-box?"

"Oh that! I'll give it to you tomorrow."

"Why tomorrow? Why not now?"

For a moment Jennings looked uneasy. "Well, actually I can't let you have it at the moment because I don't know where it is. It's bound to turn up, though."

"It had *better* turn up," Darbishire threatened. "It's my very special private possession I'll have you know. Tut! The cheek of some blokes! No respect for other people's valuable property."

The unusual sound of Jennings and Darbishire engaged in bitter argument drew Venables and Temple across from the other side of the room.

"I bet you haven't looked properly," said Temple, hoping to stir up the quarrel still further.

"Of course I have," Jennings defended himself. "I've searched all round the school, not forgetting the boiler room and behind the lockers, but it just isn't anywhere."

"What about the lost property cupboard?"

Jennings' hand shot to his mouth in guilty realisation. The lost property cupboard was the most obvious place and he'd never given it a thought. He tried to justify his lapse by saying, "I shouldn't think it'd be there. After all, everyone knows old Darbi's paint-box with that great blob of sealing-wax on the lid, so if anyone found it they'd give it back to him."

Venables nodded and said, "Ah, if one of our lot did, yes. But supposing Old Wilkie found it. He always confiscates anything that's left lying about."

As it happened, Venables' guess had hit the nail on the head. Mr Wilkins held strong views about tidiness, and on his tours of duty he would often impound articles which had not been put away in their proper places.

Three weeks ago he had come across a paint-box with a blob of sealing-wax on the lid, lying on the common-room floor while the boys were having their tea. He had treated it as lost property and tidied it away in the cupboard. After all, he reasoned, if the silly little boys hadn't got enough sense to look after their possessions they deserved to lose them. The owner could, with a little trouble, reclaim his property if he applied for it; but it was not for him – L. P. Wilkins, Esq – to waste his time hawking useless objects round the building trying to find out whom they belonged to!

"I'll go and find Sir right away," Jennings offered, jumping to his feet. He trotted across the room with Darbishire at his heels, but as he reached the door Mr Hind, the music master, came into the room and motioned to the boys to stay where they were.

Mr Hind was a tall, pale-faced man with a drawling voice who, in addition to teaching music, taught art and general subjects to the lower forms. "I'm getting a few ideas for the end of term concert," he announced when he had gained the attention of the common-room. "We've got just a month to knock some items together, so the sooner we start the better."

The concert at the end of the Christmas term was a very simple entertainment. The choir sang carols and a few boys were chosen to play piano solos or perform on the recorder.

The chief criticism voiced by the boys was that the concert was depressingly dull. Indeed, Jennings had often expressed the opinion that what was needed were some exciting items such as trick-cycling or tight-rope walking. Surely, he argued, any sensible audience would rather watch a conjuror sawing a lady in half than listen to old Rumbelow, or somebody, bashing out "The Merry Peasant" on a tinny old school piano.

His opinion was not shared by Mr Hind. "I'm putting Rumbelow and Atkinson down for a piano and violin duet," the master said, consulting a notebook he was carrying. "You should be able to manage all right, if you practise hard."

The musicians grimaced in mock terror. "Oh, sir! You know we always go wrong when we get to those difficult chords," Rumbelow protested. "Couldn't we have a drummer as well, and let Bromwich do a few loud wallops on the cymbals when we get to the tricky bits, sir?"

"Oh yes, sir!" Bromwich was only too eager to volunteer. "After all, they have drums in symphony concerts, don't they?"

Mr Hind smiled wanly and said, "Yes, but not to cover up mistakes made by the rest of the orchestra."

"The audience wouldn't know *what* it was covering up, sir," Bromwich argued. "A really fantastic thunder-storm on the kettledrums, and half the orchestra could be playing 'Land of Hope and Glory' while the rest were playing 'God Save the Queen'."

Mr Hind raised despairing eyes to the ceiling and said, "No drums, thank you very much."

Bromwich refused to give up hope.

"Well, can I sing instead then?" he pleaded. "I'm supposed to have a talent for music. My mother says my ear is very pronounced."

Temple hooted with laughter. "If my mother said my ears stuck out I'd keep quiet about it," he jeered.

The volunteer turned on him with some heat. "She didn't mean that. She was talking about my *musical* ear."

"Well, if you've got a musical ear, why don't you play a tune on it?"

It was clear that the suggestions for the concert were not being taken very seriously.

"That's enough nonsense," said Mr Hind. "If anyone's got any sensible ideas I'll listen to them; if not, keep quiet."

Jennings was not one to keep quiet.

"I'll do a solo if you like, sir," he volunteered. "Not on the piano, though – on my elastic harp."

Mr Hind winced. "On your *what*?"

"Elastic harp, sir – my own invention. It's ever so good, honestly." Proudly the inventor described the workings of his home-made, do-it-yourself instrument, the qualities of which were not yet fully recognised in the world of serious music.

"You get an old golf ball and hack the cover off, and you'll find miles and miles of elastic inside, sir," he explained. "Then you wind the elastic round something like, say, for instance, your tuckbox with the lid open, and if you start loose and end up tight you get different notes when you twang it, sir."

Darbishire had been allowed to help in the construc tion of the first prototype model and spoke up strongly in its favour. "Yes, sir, and it teaches you General Knowledge too, as well as music. I bet lots of people don't know that elastic comes from old golf balls. So if we had an orchestra of about twelve blokes with tuckboxes . . ."

But Mr Hind was not listening. In his mind's eye he could see the little stage in the gymnasium festooned from end to end with vast, throbbing spiders' webs of twisted elastic all writhing, snapping and shooting off into space.

"No, Jennings," he said firmly. "Elastic harps are 'out'. Definitely!"

By the time Mr Hind had finished discussing suggestions for the programme, it was too late fo Jennings and Darbishire to go in search of Mr Wilkin and make inquiries about the missing paint-box.

The following day Jennings raised the subjec when he handed over the table-tennis ball which he had been told to replace. But Mr Wilkins merely retorted that he was too busy at that moment to deal with lost property and would look into the matter late on . . . Whereupon he forgot all about it!

Jennings was not keen to risk a further rebuff by making a nuisance of himself, and as Darbishire had stopped pestering him, he decided to shelve the prob lem for the time being. Indeed, it was not until early the following week that his friend's missing property again became a topic of some importance.

Meanwhile, Jennings went on considering possible

tems for the concert. He was shocked at Mr Hind's vithering comments about his elastic harp. Clearly, he man didn't appreciate good music!

"There must be something else we could do," he emarked to Darbishire in the dormitory the following vening. "How would it be if, say, for instance, I kept oming on in a lot of different comic hats and told funny tories."

Darbishire sniffed. "Everybody knows your chronic, tale old jokes already: everybody's heard them at least ifty million times, so if you think . . . "

"Well, something *like* that – a real surprise item," ennings amended. "You know the sort of thing. Everyone would be sitting there expecting me to it down and play a mouldy old boring piece on he piano: and then suddenly – *hey presto* – I'd do omething that'd take their breath away, like sword-wallowing, or snake-charming, or tearing up paper to nake a model of the Eiffel Tower."

"No swords, no snakes," Darbishire objected. "We've got plenty of paper, though."

"Those are just *examples*," Jennings pointed out. "I couldn't *really* do sword-swallowing. It'd have to be omething I could learn fairly quickly like a monologue r ventriloquism or something."

Darbishire frowned in thought. "Ventriloquism! H'm, that rings a bell," he said.

"No, I don't think you can actually ring bells by it, ut you can make your voice sound as though . . . "

"I meant it rang a bell in my mind," Darbishire xplained as he screwed his shirt up into a ball and ossed it on to his bedside chair. "There's a book in the library called *The Bumper Book of Indoor Hobbies* and it's got a chapter on how to become a ventriloquist."

"Wow!" Jennings' smile was as wide as a toothpaste advertisement. Here, surely, was an item that would keep the audience sitting forward in their seats. He could picture their delight and hear their applause as, for example, a brilliant impersonation of Mr Wilkins' voice came booming out through the keyhole of the equipment cupboard in the gym, while J. C. T. Jennings, the Master Ventriloquist, stood casually examining his fingernails at the other end of the stage. It would be a sensation! . . . Then common sense came into the picture and he knew it could never be as sensational as all that! Well, not with only a month in which to perfect his art: but the idea was certainly worth trying.

"I'll get the book and start practising tomorrow," he said, tugging at a knot in his pyjama cord. "And you can help me if you like."

"Coo, thanks!"

"Yes, and we'll keep it a deadly secret. We won't let anyone know what the famous surprise item is going to be."

The entertainer and his assistant leaned across the bed and pressed their thumbs together in token of a solemn pledge of secrecy.

The door of the common-room burst open as though a small charge of dynamite had been exploded behind it, and Venables rushed into the room carrying a chess-board and a box of chess-men.

"Hey, Jennings, want to play?" he called to the

›nly other occupant who was reading at a table in a ar corner. "Rumbelow's lent me his set and there'll ust be time for a nice quiet game before tea if we get :racking."

Jennings leant forward and concealed his book with ıis arms. "No, thanks. I'm busy at the moment," he eplied.

"You're only reading; that's not being busy," /enables argued. "What's the book anyway?"

"I can't tell you. It's a secret. You'll find out n time though."

"I'll flipping well find out before then: you see f I don't."

Venables advanced to the table intending to wrest the ›ook from the reader's grasp, but instead of defending ıimself, Jennings slipped the book under his sweater, lodged round his opponent and ran out of the room.

Venables was surprised. It wasn't like old Jen o refuse a challenge to a friendly bout of all-in vrestling at any hour of the day or night. It must be ı *very* important secret that caused him to behave in his uncivilised fashion!

He put the chess-set down on the table and houted after the retreating figure: "You think you're eally clever, but I'll find out. You can't fool me like hat!"

Jennings hurried downstairs to the basement. The uck-box room was empty, so he went inside and shut he door. Peace at last, he thought. It was useless rying to practise ventriloquism in the common-room vith people charging around like bulldozers shouting heir heads off about quiet games of chess. He'd have to keep an eye on Venables, though: he had a sharp nose for ferreting out secrets and it would spoil the surprise if any hint of the sensational item was allowed to leak out before the proper time.

Jennings was not left in peace for long. Scarcely had he settled down and opened his book when Darbishire came prancing into the room to see what progress his friend was making.

"I saw you beetling downstairs, so I guessed you'd be in here," he began chattily. "How are you getting on? Can you do it yet?"

"Give me a chance," Jennings protested. "I only got the book out of the library at break. This sort of thing takes years of practice – well, weeks anyway. You see, you don't *really* throw your voice. You just make people *think* it's coming from somewhere else."

"Everybody knows that – even titchy little first-formers like Binns and Blotwell," Darbishire said scathingly. "The point is, *how* do you do it?"

"Well, supposing you want the audience to think there's a bluebottle in the room; it's no good just making a buzzing noise out of the side of your mouth."

"No?"

"You have to do the buzzing as well, of course. Like this – *zzz* – *zzz*. But the book says while you're doing it you must pretend to chase an imaginary one with a fly-swatter. That puts the idea into their heads."

"Whose heads – the bluebottles'?"

"No, you troll – the audience's."

"Oh, I see. Still, that's not actually *talking*, is it – just saying *buzz* with your mouth shut. Anyone could do that – even titchy little first-formers like Binns and Blotwell."

Jennings heaved a sigh of exasperation. "There's a lot more to it than you think," he said severely and glanced at his book for guidance. "You have to practise talking without moving your lips, even for difficult letters like *B* and *P* and *M*. I'll give you an example. Say: 'Bread and butter.'"

"Bread and butter," Darbishire replied promptly.

Jennings shook his head scornfully. "I saw your lips moving."

"Well, of course. *I'm* not learning to be a famous ventriloquist."

"OK, now watch me say it."

The assistant rubbed a grimy forefinger over his glasses to improve his vision. "Righto, I'm watching! Say 'bread and butter.'"

"Gred and gutter," the demonstrator echoed in a thick mumble.

"You cheated!" Darbishire cried accusingly. "You said 'Gred and gutter.' I heard you."

"Ah, yes, but you didn't see my lips moving – at least not much. The book says I've got to practise in front of a mirror until I can do it perfectly."

"Well, you'd better get on with it then," Darbishire retorted as the tea bell rang. "It won't be much of an act if you just chase bluebottles round the stage and woffle about bread and butter all the time."

Chapter 4

The Hitchhikers

Mr Carter paused in the doorway of the Linbury General Stores and Post Office as he heard a voice chirruping his name from the other side of the road.

Turning, he recognised little Miss Thorpe, a resident of Linbury who played a leading part in organising the social life of the village.

Miss Thorpe, neat and bird-like, swerved across the road on her bicycle and fluttered to a halt at the kerbside.

"So nice to see you again, Mr Carter," she twittered. "I was hoping I might run into you. I have a *very* special favour to ask."

Mr Carter smiled reassuringly. Whenever Miss Thorpe had a special favour to ask, the matter usually concerned the church fête, the choir outing or some other aspect of local welfare.

"It's about the parish jumble sale next Wednesday," she went on in a high-pitched trill, her eyes darting about like a robin inspecting bread crumbs. "Such an *important* event in the life of the village, I always think, and we do so depend upon it for raising funds."

"Yes, of course. Quite! Very worthy cause!" Mr Carter murmured politely.

"Well, this year, unfortunately, we're desperately short of jumble. The vicar is most concerned about it; and with the sale almost upon us, as you might say, the poor man doesn't know which way to turn."

Mr Carter expressed his sympathy over the lack of jumble and the vicar's frustrated pirouettes.

"So I told him I'd try Linbury Court," she prattled on. "Surely, I thought, in a boarding school with all those boys there are sure to be plenty of odds and ends and bits and pieces to add to our collection."

At such short notice Mr Carter couldn't think of many unwanted articles which would be of any value in stocking the stalls of a rummage sale. There was a pile of mouldering textbooks in the attic, he remembered. And, of course, it was high time that Mr Wilkins discarded his old felt slippers and bought himself a new pair. But was this worth the trouble of collecting? Mr Carter couldn't visualise the ladies of Linbury queueing up to buy out-of-date geography books or scrambling for possession of his colleague's threadbare bedroom slippers.

"I can't promise very much I'm afraid," he confessed. "But I'll have a look round when I get back to school and we'll certainly let you have anything we can find."

"Splendid! Thank you so much. The vicar *will* be pleased," she chirruped, preparing to remount her bicycle. "And it doesn't have to be anything of value, remember. We need quantity as well as quality. Any – er – unconsidered trifles, as Shakespeare says, will be more than welcome." She pressed down on the pedal, floated up to the saddle and fluttered away down the road. She reminded Mr Carter of an earnest sparrow.

During supper that evening he mentioned the parish jumble sale to his colleagues to see whether they had any suggestions to offer.

Mr Pemberton-Oakes, the headmaster, promised to donate an old radio set, Matron agreed to part with a lampshade and a plastic mac and Mr Hind offered a packet of violin strings, a scrum cap and a pair of shin-pads. These, together with Mr Wilkins' moth-eaten bedroom slippers, provided the sum total of the contributions. It was not, the headmaster admitted, a very generous donation from a school inhabited by nearly a hundred boys and staff.

"There must be some more things we could dispense with if we gave the matter a little thought," he said, frowning heavily at the coffee-pot. "Clothing, for instance, that the boys have grown out of?" He looked inquiringly at Matron, but she was unable to help as she had recently dispatched a large parcel of unwanted clothes to an organisation dealing with famine relief.

Then Mr Hind said, "How about the lost property cupboard! There's an awful lot of junk in there that'll never be claimed. Some of it's been there for years. Things belonging to boys who have left and forgotten all about it."

From across the table Mr Wilkins nodded in agreement. "Good idea! It's high time we cleared out that cupboard and got rid of the rubbish. Miss Thorpe can have the lot as far as I'm concerned."

"Don't be too ruthless, Wilkins. It wouldn't do to send her anything that's likely to be wanted again," the headmaster advised.

"Don't worry about that," his assistant assured him. "I'll have a look after supper and see what we've got."

It was a week since Mr Wilkins had inspected the collection of lost property on the first floor landing. On that occasion he had been appalled at the untidy clutter of objects piled up in a top-heavy pyramid. Since then, without his knowledge, more articles had been pushed and squeezed inside, so that now the cupboard door could only be shut with difficulty.

Unaware of the closely packed avalanche within, Mr Wilkins and Mr Carter strolled along to the cupboard when supper was over to see what could be spared for Miss Thorpe and her worthy cause.

"If you ask me, Carter, this rummage sale sounds a heaven-sent chance to get rid of a whole mountain of useless junk that's been accumulating since goodness knows when. In fact, I've a good mind to—"

As he spoke, Mr Wilkins lifted the latch . . . and then jumped back in alarm as the door catapulted on its straining hinges and the compressed contents of the cupboard cascaded out in a landslide all over the corridor.

Rolling, slithering, tumbling and overturning came tins, boxes and jam jars packed with chess-men, conkers, magnets and penknives. Tennis balls bounced, model aircraft nose-dived, and bent railway lines slid to the floor in tangled confusion. Torches, paint-boxes, jigsaw puzzles and ballpoint pens poured over the

Torches, paint-boxes, jig-saw puzzles and ball-point pens flowed like lava from a volcano.

landing like lava from a volcano, while mini-cars and locomotives skidded along the floor as far as the head of the stairs.

"*Doh*!" Mr Wilkins clapped his hand to his brow as he surveyed the scene of chaos. "Now look what's happened. Who on earth stacked these things in here like that! Disgraceful untidiness." He stepped backwards, crunching a toy signal-box beneath his left heel and treading sticks of coloured chalk into the floorboards with his right. "Tut! Just look at the mess, Carter! It looks more like a car-breaker's yard than a lost property cupboard."

Mr Carter gazed down at the tangle of mislaid possessions. "Perhaps we could sort out the stuff which belonged to boys who have left from the things which have been lost or confiscated."

"Don't be ridiculous. We'd be at it till the end of term if we did that," Mr Wilkins returned impatiently. "The only practical way is to put a selection of this rubbish into a couple of sacks or something and hope for the best."

Mr Wilkins went off to the kitchen in search of cardboard cartons in which to stack his offering for the parish jumble sale. He was delighted at the chance of making a clean sweep of so much clutter: moreover, he had no intention of allowing so vast a quantity to accumulate in the future. From henceforth, he decided, he would make sure it would be possible to open the cupboard without precipitating an avalanche all over the landing.

The lost property cupboard was cleared on Friday evening. The next morning Darbishire awoke with a feeling of misgiving. It was Saturday, the day on which he had so rashly agreed to accompany Jennings on his journey to the cleaners in Dunhambury. He had done his best to forget the whole wretched business during the last few days, but now the thought of the risks involved came flooding back into his mind, setting his nerves vibrating like harp strings. He must have been crazy to have agreed to a shrimp-witted scheme like that, he told himself! Perhaps he could persuade Jennings to abandon his plan!

But Jennings refused to be swayed by any pleas for prudence.

"It's perfectly safe, honestly," he assured his friend as they stood at the wash-basins together. "I've got the dirty clothes all done up in a brown paper parcel. And it's urgent, too. Matron will start asking where my other things are if I leave it any longer."

"Yes, but what if . . . ?"

"Oh, stop moaning, Darbi! Just leave it to me and everything will be all right. Now I'll tell you again what we're going to do . . . "

In theory the plan seemed foolproof, and indeed when it was put into practice after lunch the first stage worked smoothly enough.

As soon as the meal was over, Jennings and Darbishire scuttled downstairs to the changing-room in the basement and put on their football clothes, while the rest of the school sat down with library books for the daily rest period which was held immediately after lunch. There was little chance that their absence would be noticed at this stage, for the master on duty would assume that anyone who wasn't in the library would be reading in the common-room farther along the corridor.

Jennings glanced at his watch as he scrambled into his football shirt. "Hurry up, Darbi! The bus goes in five minutes and you haven't got your boots on yet."

"I don't like wearing my football boots in the street. The studs make you walk like a cat on hot bricks. Couldn't I change when we get back?"

"No, you definitely couldn't! There won't be time. The whole point of getting ready first is so's we can nip straight on to the pitch as though we'd just come out with the rest of the blokes." Jennings picked up the brown-paper parcel containing his soiled sweater and trousers. "Come on, I'm ready now. How much longer are you going to be!"

It was three minutes before the bus was due when the pair, wearing raincoats over their football clothes, slipped out of the changing-room and crept towards the side door of the building. On their way they had to pass the staff room, and as they neared the door they heard the telephone bell ringing inside the room.

They stopped dead in their tracks. If the bell should bring some master hurrying down the stairs to answer its summons . . . ! But all was well. Beyond the closed door the telephone stopped ringing and they heard Mr Carter speaking into the mouthpiece.

"Linbury Court here! . . . Who did you say? . . . Oh, Bracebridge School! Hello, Parkinson, how are you!"

Jennings and Darbishire tiptoed past the door in their ungainly footwear. Mr Carter's conversation was no business of theirs, and if it served to distract his attention from what was going on in the hall, so much the better!

Unobserved, they made their way out through the side door, scuttled across the kitchen yard and took shelter in the bushes beyond. They felt safer then, for the shrubbery ran parallel with the drive and provided cover all the way down to the gate. Tense with excitement, they scurried through the undergrowth and darted through the entrance on to the main road.

Then came the first setback. As they emerged through the gate, a green double-decker bus shot past at forty miles an hour travelling towards the request stop some fifty yards farther along the Dunhambury road.

"Oh, fish-hooks, we've missed it!" cried Darbishire.

"No we haven't. It'll wait at the stop."

Jennings raced along the road after the bus waving his free arm and shouting to attract the conductor's attention. But all in vain. There was no one waiting at the request stop and the driver didn't even bother to slow down. When the would-be passengers reached the stop a few seconds later, the vehicle had rounded the bend and disappeared from sight.

"Coo! Mouldy chizzle. Rotten old mouldy chizz! That bus was running early," he fumed as Darbishire cantered up to join him. To prove his point Jennings thrust his wrist-watch under his friend's nose so violently that Darbishire's glasses were knocked askew. "Look at that! There's still at least a minute before it's due."

"Perhaps your watch is wrong. The school clock's always a bit slow by the radio."

"I put it right by the one o'clock pips. This isn't school time – it's Greenwich pip-pip-pip Mean Time, so that proves the bus was early. He might have had the decency to wait."

Jennings' tone was bitter, for this turn of events had completely wrecked his plans. If they waited half an hour for the next bus, they could not possibly get back to school in time for football practice and their absence would certainly be noticed.

"Yes, of course. Triple rotten shame," Darbishire sympathised. He did his best to sound disappointed, though secretly he was relieved that this spine-chilling nightmare of a scheme must now be abandoned. "Still, that old bus-driver's bished up the issue properly, so all we can do in the meantime – or rather in the Greenwich pipping Mean Time, I should say . . . " He broke off and giggled at his little joke. "All we can do is to call the whole thing off and get back into school again without being spotted."

With this in mind, he was about to cross the road when he saw a small grey car coming towards them, travelling in the same direction as the bus. Mindful of kerb drill, he waited on the footpath for it to go by.

Jennings, however, had other ideas. As the car approached he raised his hand like a hitchhiker thumbing a lift. It was a forlorn, despairing gesture and he had no real hope that the motorist would pay any attention. But to his surprise (and Darbishire's dismay) the car pulled up a few yards beyond the bus stop.

Jennings danced along the road after it in glee. It was going to be all right after all!

The car door opened and an attractive young woman in her early twenties looked out and said, "I can take you as far as Dunhambury if that's any use."

"Coo, thanks! That'd be fabulous," Jennings replied, skidding to a halt beside the open door. "We missed the bus, you see, and we're in a frantic hurry because – because . . . " It would be unwise to reveal secret and confidential plans to a complete stranger, he thought, even though she looked so friendly. " . . . because we haven't got much time."

She laughed and invited them to jump in the back. She was travelling alone and was pleased to have company for the five-mile journey to the market town. "So you're off to play football!" she said, noticing their boots, and the quartered shirts poking through their clumsily-buttoned raincoats.

"Well, yes, but not at Dunhambury. We've got to get there and back before the game starts," Jennings explained. And then, as she still seemed interested he found himself telling her the true story of their expedition as the car sped along the road. She was a sympathetic listener and didn't laugh when he described his dive into the ditch and their nerve-wracking experience behind the hedge with Mr Wilkins within earshot. She even seemed to understand why it was so important to keep their escapade from coming to the ears of the staff.

" . . . and so when we missed the bus we were going to call the whole thing off," Jennings finished up. "And then you came along like a fairy godmother out of a pantomime and made everything all right again."

The fairy godmother laughed and said, "It's a bit

soon to say that. You're not home yet! Still, I'll keep my fingers crossed for you."

They had reached the town by now and she stopped the car in the High Street for the boys to alight before continuing her journey.

"Thanks ever so much for the lift," Darbishire said as he stepped out on to the pavement. He was feeling a little happier by this time. Although still ill at ease, he took comfort from the fact that their dangerous mission had the moral support of such a friendly fairy godmother.

"Yes, rather. Thank you very much," Jennings echoed. "I don't know what we should have done without you."

They waved as the car moved off and then made their way towards the Express Dry Cleaning Company on the other side of the road.

"She *was* fantastic, wasn't she," Jennings remarked as he led the way into the shop and put his brown paper parcel on the counter. "I'm ever so glad we met her."

"And *I'm* ever so glad she's keeping her fingers crossed," Darbishire replied solemnly. "If you ask me, we're going to need all the good luck we can get before we're through with this caper."

Chapter 5

Web of Crossed Purposes

At about the same moment that Jennings was chasing the elusive bus along the Dunhambury road, Mr Carter, having finished his telephone call, was talking to the headmaster and Mr Wilkins in the hall outside the staff room.

"Bracebridge have just rung up to see if we can fit in that fixture we had to scratch," he told them. "It's rather short notice, but we haven't got anything important arranged for this afternoon, so I said we'd be over in time for a three o'clock kick-off."

The headmaster nodded in approval. Earlier in the term a second XI match against the opposing school had been postponed because of the waterlogged condition of the home side's football pitch. Today, with a light breeze blowing and a hint of sunshine in the sky, would provide a good opportunity for the game to be played.

"I'll tell the team to get ready straight away and we'll make a dash for the ten-past-two bus," Mr Carter went on. "How about you, Wilkins? Would you like to come along as well?"

"Yes, I should," his colleague agreed. "We're cutting it a bit fine, though. You know how long it takes some of those silly little boys to get changed with all those knots in their bootlaces and missing garters and what-have-you."

The headmaster glanced at his watch. "That's all right. I shall be going into Dunhambury by car within the next hour, so I'll pick up any stragglers you have to leave behind. I'll put them down at the bus shelter in the High Street and you can collect them from there."

The quickest way to assemble the team was to make an announcement in the library and the common-room where all the boys concerned were supposed to be seated during the compulsory rest period.

Mr Wilkins volunteered for this duty. In both rooms he boomed out the altered arrangements for the afternoon and read out the list of boys playing in the team and the linesman accompanying the side.

The news was greeted with enthusiasm by ten of the twelve boys whose names were read out. Scampering down to the changing-room they threw off their day clothes and scrambled into football shirts and shorts.

The other two boys whose names had been called were deaf to the summons . . . And this was not surprising for Jennings (right half) and Darbishire (linesman) were at that moment speeding along the Dunhambury road in a small grey car driven by an obliging fairy godmother.

Matron was crossing the hall as Mr Wilkins came downstairs from his room buttoning his overcoat and fumbling in his pocket for his gloves.

"I hear you're off to Bracebridge!" she greeted him. "I wonder if you'd have time to do me a favour and get me a tin of *Puss-Ee-Kins*."

"Tin of What-*Ee-Kins*?" he queried. It sounded an undignified commodity to ask for in a shop.

"Cat food: for George the Third. I shan't have time to get in to the village before the shops close."

George the Third was a large, ginger-coloured tom-cat that spent most of his life sunning himself on the library window ledge or dozing in front of the gas fire in Matron's sitting-room. The animal was not related to the royal House of Hanover, and his regal title sprang from the fact that he belonged to the third generation of ginger-coloured cats which Matron had cared for during the past few years.

"We're in a bit of a rush," Mr Wilkins demurred. "We shan't have much time in Dunhambury before the kick-off, but I'll do my best."

"Thank you so much. There's a shop down that side street close to the bus shelter where they always stock it. But don't bother if you haven't time. There's sure to be someone else going into town."

"All right, Matron. I'll see what I can do." Mr Wilkins flashed her a bright smile and hurried down to the changing-room to make sure that the team were not wasting their time in idle chatter.

At five minutes past two Mr Carter and Mr Wilkins shepherded a group of footballers down the drive on the first stage of their journey to Dunhambury. Bracebridge School was situated on the outskirts of the town, a short walk from the bus stop in the High Street.

As the team passed through the main gate, Mr Carter said, "Did you check to see they're all here, Wilkins?"

"No, actually I didn't. There was too much of a last-minute rush going on." Mr Wilkins ran his eye over the straggling group and his brow creased in a frown. "That's funny! We seem to be two short. There ought to be twelve, including the linesman."

"Linesman! Ah, yes, of course, where's Darbishire?" queried Mr Carter. "And Jennings too? Neither of them is here."

Venables, trotting along at the masters' side, said, "They'll miss the bus, won't they, sir! Oughtn't someone to go back and find them?"

"There isn't time. It's due any moment now."

"But, sir, that means we shall have to play one man short. It doesn't matter about the linesman so much, but we can't do without . . . "

"It's all right, Venables. Don't worry," Mr Carter assured him. "The headmaster's arranged to pick up anyone who wasn't ready when we left. He's going to take them along in his car."

"Coo, lucky old them! I wish I was going by car. I shouldn't be surprised if they get to Dunhambury before we do."

His observation had a ring of truth about it: for as the team were taking their seats on the bus, the two absentees were disappearing through the doorway of the Express Dry Cleaning Company in Dunhambury High Street.

The manageress of the dry cleaners was most helpful.

She agreed to dispatch the garments by parcel post addressed to her young customer personally, and to send the account to his parents for payment.

Satisfied, the young customer and his friend left the shop. So far the plan was running smoothly. Provided they caught the two-twenty-five bus back to school and could slip undetected on to the football pitch, *Operation Dry Cleaning* might well be looked upon as one of Jennings' more successful achievements.

They were in no hurry, for the bus was not due to depart for a quarter of an hour. So they strolled along the High Street gazing at the shop windows, enjoying the forbidden freedom of mixing with the Saturday afternoon shoppers. Suddenly, Jennings grabbed Darbishire's arm and pulled him into the shelter of a shop doorway.

"What's up?" Darbishire gibbered in alarm.

"It's the Head! I just saw his car going down the street."

"Oh, fish-hooks! Did he see us?"

"No, he was watching the traffic. Still, he may stop somewhere and get out, so we'd better go and take cover behind the bus shelter, just to be on the safe side."

The narrow escape brought all Darbishire's fears flooding back again. His throat went dry and there was an empty feeling in the pit of his stomach.

"Oh, goodness, we should never have done this!" he quavered. "Supposing he'd seen us! Supposing he comes back again! Supposing . . . "

"It's all *right*, I tell you," Jennings assured him as they threaded their way past the perambulators blocking the pavement and the bicycles parked by the kerb. "He was all alone in the car and he went on past the traffic lights, so he can't possibly know we're here."

As they approached the shelter they saw a bus drawing to a halt at the stop. Darbishire, still flustered, darted ahead saying, "Come on! It's in. Let's get on quick!"

Jennings laid a restraining hand upon his friend's arm. "You're bonkers! That one's going the wrong way," he pointed out. "It's just *come* from Linbury."

"Oh, yes, of course! We want the stop on the other side of the road, don't we."

"It's about time you pulled yourself together, Darbi. You're getting all jittery again," Jennings said severely. "Just keep calm and leave everything . . . "

His words died away, and he stared in speechless horror at the double-decker which had just drawn up. For the first passenger to alight on to the pavement was L. P. Wilkins, Esq.

Darbishire had seen him too. Panic-stricken, the two boys turned and dived into a side street running at right angles to the main road. Here, there was no obvious hiding place and the only method of concealment was to seek refuge in the nearest shop.

Jennings didn't hesitate. Seizing Darbishire by the wrist, he dragged him in through the door of an emporium dedicated to the sale of hardware, pet food and a wide variety of household goods. Tense with alarm, they came to rest beside a pyramid of tinned cats'-meat displayed in the centre of the shop. There were several customers making purchases and all the assistants were busy, so for a few minutes at any rate they had a breathing space in which to take stock of the spine-chilling predicament in which they were placed.

"Oh, my goodness, this is terrible," gasped Darbishire. "You don't think Sir saw us, do you?"

For the second time in five minutes Jennings was able to give a reassuring reply. "No, I'm sure he didn't. We were round the corner before he had time to blink."

"I thought I saw someone in a school cap getting off, too," Darbishire said uncertainly. "It looked like Atkinson or somebody."

"You couldn't have done. Must be your nerves. All these masters popping up from nowhere have given you optical illusions. What on earth would Atki be doing in Dunhambury?"

"Well, if it comes to that, what's Old Wilkie doing here?"

"Just stonking around. Masters often do. The only safe thing is to stay here for a few minutes to give him time to push off to wherever he's going."

"But we'll miss the bus!" cried Darbishire, aghast.

Jennings shrugged. "We'll have to take the next one and chance it. It'd be asking for trouble to go out into the street now."

By this time two or three customers had left the shop, and it was clear that it would soon be the boys' turn to be served.

"We can't afford to buy anything, remember. We've only just enough for our bus fares," Jennings cautioned. "So when they ask what we want, we'll have to say something that they haven't got. Something impossible like a – like a —" He looked about him for inspiration. Just ahead of him in the queue, a customer wearing shiny black wellingtons was buying a metal paraffin funnel. Jennings juggled the objects in his mind and went on: " . . . like elastic-sided wellington boots or an ear-trumpet."

"What would I want with elastic-sided wellington boots?"

"Don't be so feeble, Darbi. You don't have to *buy* them. You just have to *ask* for them. Even if they'd got them, you could always make out they were the wrong size."

"Yes, of course," Darbishire agreed. "I could pretend I've got extra small feet, couldn't I?"

"Or extra large ears. You wouldn't have to pretend about that: they could see for themselves."

The man in the wellingtons picked up his change and his funnel and moved away from the counter. The shop assistant, a middle-aged lady in a green overall, turned inquiringly to the next customers.

"Good afternoon," said Jennings. "Have you any elastic-sided wellington boots?"

"Or extra large ear-trumpets?" Darbishire added hopefully.

She leaned farther over the counter. "Speak up a bit, ducks. I'm a bit hard of hearing."

"I said, 'Have you got an ear-trumpet?'" Darbishire repeated loudly.

"No, ducks, I don't need one. Just speak clearly, that's all. What was it you wanted?"

They didn't stock elastic-sided wellington boots,

she told them, but if they wouldn't mind waiting a minute, she thought they'd got some wellingtons of a more conventional pattern outside in the stock room.

Jennings turned to Darbishire with a satisfied smile as she disappeared into the room behind the shop. This was going to be a good time-wasting manoeuvre to delay their departure until the coast was clear.

The next minute the smile froze on his face as the door swung open and Mr Wilkins strode into the shop in search of cat food.

Jennings' jaw dropped and his hand shot to his mouth in startled confusion. They were caught red-handed without a shred of excuse to explain their unlawful activities.

Darbishire, goggling like a goldfish, was so panic-stricken that he gave a guilty start and knocked a tin of *Puss-Ee-Kins* off the display stand.

In a whirl of mental blankness he unconsciously picked it up and stood holding it out like a peace-offering to an avenging foe. In silence they waited for the storm of indignation to break from Mr Wilkins' outraged lips . . . But, oddly enough, it didn't!

Instead, he threw them a casual glance of recognition and said, "Oh, so there you are! I was expecting to find you waiting at the bus shelter." Then he noticed the tin of cat food in Darbishire's hand. "So Matron asked you too, did she! She obviously didn't think I'd have time."

The boys stared at him in astonishment. Had Mr Wilkins taken leave of his senses? . . . Had the shock of unmasking such a dastardly crime unhinged his mind? Considering the facts, he should be quivering

Darbishire, goggling like a goldfish was panic-stricken.

with anger and prophesying punishments . . . And instead of that, here was Old Wilkie chatting to them as calmly as though he was passing the time of day in the common-room. It was fantastic . . . unbelievable!

"Just as well we arranged for you slow people to come along by car," Mr Wilkins went on pleasantly. "Buses, like time and tide, wait for no man."

Jennings and Darbishire were baffled. How could Sir have known about the non-stopping bus and the helpful motorist? And if he *did* know, why wasn't he furious? In the circumstances their bewilderment was natural, for they knew nothing of the altered arrangements and the headmaster's offer to give a lift to the laggards.

Mr Wilkins took the cat food from Darbishire's trembling fingers. "H'm! Hope this is the right stuff. Doesn't look too appetising, does it?"

"Oh! I wasn't going to buy it, sir, honestly," Darbishire faltered. "It's *Puss-Ee-Kins*, sir. Specially for cats. It says so on the tin."

"Well, of *course* it's for cats. I didn't think it was rhinoceros food. It's what you came in for, isn't it, so why sound so shattered about it?"

Darbishire was saved from further explanations by the hard-of-hearing shop assistant who came back at that moment to announce that she was unable to help them in their quest for elastic-sided wellington boots.

This time it was Mr Wilkins who looked baffled. "Elastic-sided *what*?" he queried.

"Wellington boots," she repeated. "These lads here were inquiring about them. And ear-trumpets, too."

"*Ear-trumpets*!"

"Yes, but we don't sell those either. Ever so sorry!"

Mr Wilkins placed a coin on the counter and slipped the tin of *Puss-Ee-Kins* into his pocket. He'd no idea what the silly little boys had been up to, but whatever it was, explanations would have to wait until later.

"Come along, you boys," he said, leading the way out into the street. "We shall have to hurry up or you'll be late for the game."

"Game, sir?" Jennings echoed in puzzled wonder. "What game, sir?"

"Don't talk such nonsense," Mr Wilkins said sharply. "You haven't changed into your football clothes in order to play tiddley-winks, have you!"

"You mean we're going to play *football*, sir?"

Was the boy mad, Mr Wilkins wondered? Or was he trying to be funny? No one – not even Jennings — could be so dim-witted, unless he had taken leave of his senses.

"What on earth's the matter with you?" the master demanded as they set off up the street towards the main road. "You wouldn't be here at all if you weren't playing in the match against Bracebridge, would you!"

Jennings looked at him in round-eyed surprise. "Oh, is there a match today, sir? Sorry, sir, I didn't know."

Mr Wilkins was so astounded that he stopped dead and gaped at the boys as though they were some strange biological specimens hitherto unknown to science.

"You didn't know!" he echoed weakly.

"No, sir. We didn't hear anything about a match."

"But this is fantastic!" Mr Wilkins cried, doing a

little morris dance of exasperation on the pavement. "You change into your football clothes, and you're given a lift into the town, and now you turn round and tell me you don't know what you're here for! I've never heard such asinine tomfoolery in my life. If you didn't know there was a match this afternoon, what in the name of thunder do you imagine you've come all the way to Dunhambury for?"

Jennings' mind was spinning with bewilderment. The web of misunderstanding was now so tangled that he didn't know which of their misdeeds Mr Wilkins knew about, and which he didn't. In this topsy-turvy situation, when any chance remark was liable to give the game away, the only thing to do was make a clean breast of the whole affair.

"Well, sir, what happened was this. You see, we wanted to get some dry cleaning done – privately, without worrying Matron," he began. "Only, actually, it really started before that when Darbishire and I went to play ping-pong and . . . "

But at that moment the town hall clock started to chime the hour and they were still five minutes' walk from the Bracebridge football ground.

"All right, all right! I haven't got time to listen to a long rigmarole of nonsense," Mr Wilkins broke in. Placing a hand on each boy's shoulder, he propelled them up the street at a brisk six miles an hour. "Come along, for goodness' sake. The match will be half over before we get there at this rate."

Jennings and Darbishire trotted along beside him in thankful silence, but Mr Wilkins, impatient and exasperated, continued to give voice to a somewhat confused monologue about the stupidity of boys in general and the events of the last five minutes in particular.

"Tut! Ping-pong! . . . Cat food! . . . Puss-in-dry-cleaned-wellington-boots! . . . Elastic-sided ear-trumpets!" they heard him mumbling beneath his breath. "Must need their heads seeing to. I've never heard such ridiculous poppycock in all my life!"

The match against Bracebridge ended in a goal-less draw. Jennings played a reliable game at right half without distinguishing himself in any way, and Darbishire managed not to make too many mistakes when deciding which side had earned the advantage of the throw-in.

The headmaster arrived shortly after half-time, having finished his business in the town, and stayed to watch the rest of the match. When the team was ready to leave and had said goodbye to their opponents he called for their attention and said, "I've got room for a couple of boys in the back of my car. Who'd like to come?"

Twelve hands shot skywards. Everyone agreed that a ride home in a master's car was better than a slow journey on the bus.

Mr Pemberton-Oakes looked at the forest of upraised hands. "No, not you Venables; nor you Temple. I gave you a lift only last week. It's time someone else had a turn." His gaze came to rest upon the right half and the linesman standing at the back of the group. "I'll take Jennings and Darbishire. I haven't had the – ah – the pleasure of their company on a journey for quite a long time."

No one questioned this surprising remark out loud, for one does not argue with headmasters. But the remainder of the team and both masters exchanged puzzled glances as Mr Pemberton-Oakes and his two passengers climbed into the car and shot off in a swirl of exhaust smoke.

"Bonkers! The Archbeako must be stark raving bonkers," Temple muttered to Venables. "Talk about absent-minded! It's less than a couple of hours since he gave those two a lift, and he's forgotten about it already."

Venables sighed enviously. "Lucky old them! Some blokes get jam on everything."

The two passengers in the headmaster's car might well have disputed Temple's version of the story while agreeing with Venables' summing-up.

They *had* been lucky! In spite of the misadventures which had befallen them during the afternoon, Fortune had also smiled in their direction . . .

Wonderful to relate, *Operation Dry Cleaning* had been carried through without the full facts of the project coming to light!

Chapter 6

Gred and Gutter Practice

On Monday Darbishire remembered his paint-box. The thought came to him in the middle of Mr Hind's scripture class, and as soon as the lesson was over he took Jennings to task for his negligence during the past few days.

"Honestly, you are a ruin, Jen! That paint-box was my favourite private possession, I'll have you know. My godmother gave it to me for . . . "

"All right, all right," his friend protested. "You've told me that a hundred-and-forty-nine million times already."

"Well, now I'm telling you for the hundred-and-fifty millionth. You promised to see Old Wilkie about it last week."

"I was busy," Jennings defended himself. "I'd got my muddy sweater on my mind and besides that I had my ventriloquism practice. I'm getting on quite well now. I can say, '*Stop mumbling and pass the bread and butter please, Humphrey*' ever so well without my lips moving. It's one of the exercises. And you should just hear my bluebottles! They're fabulous! And as for my imitation of a man sawing wood, I'd defy anyone to tell where the noise was coming from."

Darbishire dismissed the progress report with an impatient wave of his hand. On some more suitable occasion he would be delighted to listen for hours on end to a whole plague of non-existent bluebottles or a complete sawmill in action, but at the moment he had something else to think about. "Come on, let's go straight away. We've got ten minutes before the end of break."

The lost property cupboard was never locked – the key having disappeared several terms before – but the boys were not allowed access to it without obtaining a master's permission. With this in mind they scurried off to find a member of the staff, and were just passing the cupboard when they met Mr Carter approaching along the corridor from the opposite direction.

"Sir, please, sir! May we have permish to have a look," Jennings called out, jerking his thumb at the door. "Darbishire's lost something, sir."

"Well, I like the cheek of that," Darbishire protested. "It's not *me* that lost it, sir – it's Jennings! I lent it to him and he went and left it lying about on my behalf, as you might say."

Mr Carter suggested that it might simplify matters if he could be informed of the nature of the loss.

"Oh, sorry, sir. It's my paint-box," Darbishire explained. "It's a big black tin one with a large blob of red sealing-wax on the lid so's everyone will know it's mine. You haven't seen it, have you?"

As it happened, Mr Carter *had* seen it. He remembered a blob of red sealing-wax on one of the paint-boxes that had come cascading out of the cupboard the previous Friday evening.

Jennings was delighted with this information. "There you are, you see, Darbi, it's quite safe. I knew I hadn't lost it. Actually it's a whole heap safer in the cupboard than anywhere else, really." He turned again to Mr Carter. "May we have it then, please, sir?"

"You can look, but you may be unlucky." Mr Carter opened the door and revealed a small collection of useful objects neatly arranged on the shelves. But of the vast quantity of odds and ends which had previously filled the cupboard from floor to ceiling there was no sign. Mr Wilkins had done his job thoroughly.

Darbishire ran his eye over the shelves. "Where is it, sir?" he demanded. "You said it was in here, but I can't see it."

"I said it was in there *last week*," Mr Carter corrected. "And if you'd claimed it then, you could have had it. Unfortunately for you, Mr Wilkins made a grand clearance at the weekend and got rid of most of the clutter."

"Oh, but, sir, I *must* have it back," Darbishire protested. "It's my most important private possession."

"I'm sorry, Darbishire, but you should have asked for it before," Mr Carter sympathised. He felt annoyed with his colleague for being so ruthless, and yet it was understandable, for the incident was typical of youthful carelessness in looking after personal belongings. "Why don't you pay attention when lost property announcements are being given out?"

"But I didn't *know* I'd lost it. I thought Jennings had got it."

Darbishire looked so woebegone that Jennings was stricken with a bad attack of conscience. It was all his fault, he told himself. He must do what he could to put matters right before it was too late. Hopefully, he turned to Mr Carter and asked, "Do you know where Mr Wilkins has taken all these things, sir?"

"Yes, they've gone to the parish hall for a jumble sale on Wednesday."

Jennings looked puzzled. "Jungle sale, sir? You mean, elephants and things?" It seemed an odd place to sell a second-hand paint-box.

"No, Jennings, not *jungle*. Jumble sale, rummage sale – call it what you like."

Jennings thought for a moment and said, "Well, sir, if there's village leave on Wednesday do you think we could go to this rumble sale and . . . "

Mr Carter tut-tutted patiently. "Rummage *or* jumble, Jennings. You can't combine the two."

"No, sir, I only want to go to one of them. The one where Darbishire's paint-box has gone, so I can buy it back for him."

The request was unusual, but there was no valid reason why it should be refused. Although the boys were seldom permitted to visit Dunhambury without an escort, they were often allowed into the village on half-holidays if this did not interfere with school routine.

"All right, then," Mr Carter agreed. "Though I must say it seems a bit silly to give something to a jumble sale and then rush down and buy it back."

"But *we* didn't give it, sir – Mr Wilkins did," Jennings pointed out with flawless logic.

"True! And if it was your own paint-box, Jennings, I'd say it served you right for not looking after it. But as you've been careless with someone else's property, it may teach you a lesson if you have to pay for it."

The jumble sale was due to start at three o'clock on Wednesday afternoon. Mr Carter had seen a poster to this effect in the Linbury Stores, and he warned the boys that, as they would not be allowed out until after football practice, they might well find upon arrival that the sale was over and the article disposed of to some other purchaser.

"We'll have to risk that, sir," Jennings remarked, as the bell rang for the end of break. "After all, I don't suppose many of those old women you see stonking about in the village would want Darbishire's paint-box as a gift – let alone pay for it."

Mr Carter had only one other piece of advice to offer. As the boys turned to retrace their steps along the corridor he said, "By the way, Jennings, mind you buy it back with your own money and not with Darbishire's!"

Jennings looked at Mr Carter with an expression of shocked surprise. "Oh, *sir*!" he said in reproachful tones. "As though I'd do a thing like *that*, sir! As though I *would*!"

It is not easy to become an expert ventriloquist, even when one is free to practise out loud without restraint. But trying to learn the art secretly in public surroundings is an almost impossible task.

Boarding school was a hopeless place for anyone seeking a quiet spot for private rehearsals, Jennings decided. There just wasn't anywhere to go. Every time he settled down with his book to do his vocal exercises, some inquisitive colleague would come and sit beside him, obliging him to conceal the volume under his stamp album which he carried about with him for that purpose.

Venables in particular caused the would-be ventriloquist a great deal of trouble, for he took such a suspicious interest in his desire for privacy that Jennings had been forced to hide *The Bumper Book of Indoor Hobbies* in a different place every day since taking up his studies just over a week before.

In spite of these difficulties, he persisted with his practice whenever he found an opportunity. In the dormitory he would spend time in front of the mirror asking Humphrey for the bread and butter (*Exercise 3*) until he felt sure that the movement of his lips could not be detected. Outside on the football field the drone of winged insects, the popping of corks and the grating noise of a saw cutting logs (*Exercise 2*) came rasping out of the corner of his mouth as he ran about the pitch.

Once or twice he tried out his powers on unsuspecting friends, hoping to baffle them without revealing the source of the mystery.

But the results were disappointing. On Monday afternoon, for example, when Bromwich was going upstairs, Jennings put on his special ventriloquial voice and said, "Hey there! You've dropped your handkerchief, you half-baked nut case."

In theory, Bromwich should have looked about him in surprise seeking some clue to the body-less voice from nowhere, and never suspecting that the sound could have come from the bored-looking figure polishing his fingernails in the hall below.

Instead, the victim looked down and said, "You're bonkers, Jennings. I haven't even *got* a handkerchief – let alone dropped one. What are you croaking for, anyway? Sore throat, or something?"

And on Tuesday the odd behaviour of the aspiring performer caused Mr Wilkins to feel worried on the boy's behalf. He mentioned the matter to Mr Carter in the staff room shortly after tea.

"Frankly, Carter, I think the lad has gone completely off his head," he remarked in the tone of resigned bewilderment in which he so often discussed the members of Form Three. "He's been doing the most extraordinary things for some days now."

"More extraordinary than usual?" Mr Carter asked, looking up from the essay he was marking.

"Oh, yes. I came across him all alone in the wash-room yesterday, making faces at himself in the mirror," Mr Wilkins went on. "He was grunting and mumbling through clenched teeth as though he'd got a mouthful of cotton-wool. Kept muttering about someone called Humphrey. And when I asked him what he was playing at, he said that if we both listened carefully we might hear somebody sawing logs in the broom cupboard."

Mr Carter smiled reassuringly. Alarming though the symptoms might sound, he knew from experience that growing boys often indulged in fanciful games of make-believe, puzzling to those of riper years. "He'll get over it!" he said.

"Well, he's not showing much sign of getting over it yet. In fact, he's getting worse if you ask me." Mr

Wilkins edged his chair six inches nearer and fixed his colleague with the serious look of one who has incredible news to impart. "Believe it or not, Carter, I went into the dining-hall just before tea today, and there he was dancing round the tables making wild swipes at the empty air with a rolled-up newspaper."

Mr Carter nodded gravely. "And what explanation did he offer for that?"

"He said – " Mr Wilkins paused to visualise the scene in his mind's eye – "He said there was a bluebottle on the bread and butter."

"Really!" Mr Carter sounded suprised. Bluebottles were rare in November.

"Well, actually that's not *quite* what he said," his colleague amended. After all, he wanted to be fair to the boy and get the facts right. "His actual words were: 'There's a gluegottle on the gred and gutter'."

"H'm!" Mr Carter looked thoughtful. "And there wasn't, of course?"

"Wasn't what?"

"A bluebottle on the bread and butter."

"Don't be ridiculous, Carter! Of *course* there wasn't," Mr Wilkins retorted impatiently. "There was jam on some pieces and potted meat on the others. There wasn't a gluegottle – er, I mean a bluebottle anywhere in the room."

The bell rang for the start of prep and Mr Wilkins rose and made his way to the door.

"Sawing logs in the broom cupboard! . . . Bluebottles on the tea table!" he muttered as he left the room. "Tut–tut–tut! What on earth will the silly little boy be thinking up next!"

Chapter 7

Sale or Return

The county guide-book refers to the village of Linbury as an agricultural community with a population of three hundred and ninety-eight. It mentions the early Norman church and the late Victorian horse-trough, but says nothing about the social activities of the inhabitants.

This is a serious omission, for although it would be an exaggeration to describe Linbury as a hub of culture, there is no doubt that a strong community feeling prevails on alternate Wednesdays in the winter months when jumble sales, whist drives and similar functions are held in the parish hall under the auspices of Miss Thorpe.

Other villages may boast of quaint customs dating back to medieval times. Some are renowned for maypole dances, pancake races or knocking on neighbours' doors at midnight with the jawbones of dead horses. In Linbury, the parish jumble sale, though dating from a later period in history, has achieved the reputation of being the most perilous and exhausting event in the rural calendar.

Those attending the sale are well aware of the possible danger to life and limb. Local experts reckon the chance of survival to be midway between the risks of ski-jumping and the hazards of mixed hockey – to both of which sports the Linbury jumble sale bears some resemblance.

At three o'clock when the door is unbolted, a solid phalanx of Linbury ladies stampedes into the building, overturning the card table by the door where the vicar is feebly trying to collect their entrance money. With shrill cries in the local dialect they advance upon the merchandise laid out upon the tables with the determination of the Assyrian coming down like a wolf on the fold.

For a time confusion reigns as purchasers wrestle for possession of eiderdowns, egg-cosies, horror-comics and plaster busts of King Edward VII, while Miss Thorpe and her sales people do their best to collect the cash, guard the stock and keep a watchful eye on the takings in the cocoa-tin on the window-sill.

At the clothing stall the chaos is always considerable. Overalls, coats, dresses and well-worn gardening trousers are wrenched from hand to hand or waved like a matador's cloak in a bullring as a challenge to a frontal attack: while at the footwear table across the room, crépe-soled sandals and odd gym-shoes skim over the heads of the crowd like boomerangs on an Aboriginal battlefield.

Customers who force their way through to the sundry utensils department have an advantage over their fellows. For here they can buy a rickety perambulator, a garden roller or a brass-knobbed bedstead and use their purchases as battering-rams and bulldozers to clear a gangway back to the entrance.

After twenty minutes of gruelling activity all the best bargains have been sold, and the pace slackens to little more than the rough and tumble of an average rugger match.

Then, at about three forty-five p.m. the mood changes. Still game, but gasping with exhaustion, the ladies of Linbury sink down onto any chairs that have survived the mêlée and regain their strength with tea (*30p per cup—biscuits 10p extra*).

Chatter round the tea-urn continues for about an hour, after which the satisfied customers go home, leaving Miss Thorpe and her helpers to sweep up the wreckage of yet another red-letter day in the history of the social and cultural life of the village.

This, then, was the procedure at the jumble sale which Jennings and Darbishire had been given permission to attend, but as they were not allowed to leave school until after football practice, they were spared the early stages of the fray when the hurly-burly was at its height.

"I only hope it won't be over before we get there," Darbishire said anxiously as he hurried along the field footpath beside his friend. "I could hardly wait for the final whistle, thinking of my paint-box on sale to the public without me being there to stop it. Why, a valuable piece of property like that might be snapped up in a matter of seconds."

"We'll soon know," replied Jennings, forcing the pace a little faster. "And if it *has* been sold, don't blame me. Blame Old Wilkie; it's all his doing."

"It's your fault, too, don't forget!" Darbishire felt strongly on this matter. "What with blokes like you borrowing blokes' things and losing them, and blokes like Old Wilkie giving other blokes' things away without asking, it's not safe for a bloke to let his private possessions out of his sight unless he goes too, to keep an eye on them." He sighed. "I've a good mind to complain if I could only find someone who'd listen."

By this time they had left the field path and were making their way along the village street. Just ahead of them they could see the parish hall with a poster attached to the notice board outside: *Jumble Sale Today. Admission 20p.*

"Twenty pence! Coo, mouldy chizz. Fancy having to pay to go in and get your own things back," Darbishire grumbled. A thought struck him and he said, "I wonder if they make reductions for school parties of not less than two people."

But there was no one at the door to take their money, for the vicar had retired to the kitchen at the back of the hall in the hope of finding an aspirin and a cup of tea. It was twenty minutes to four, the bulk of the afternoon's buying was over and the ladies were just beginning to crowd round the tea-urn with a thirsty look in their eyes.

Across the room, Miss Thorpe was grappling with a bamboo plant in a garden tub and looking like a tired starling trying to carry a large twig back to its nest.

Jennings and Darbishire went across and helped her. They had met Miss Thorpe at the church fête in the summer when, for the best of reasons, Jennings had entered a cake baked by his aunt for a cookery competition.

Miss Thorpe seemed pleased to see them again, and when the wobbling bamboo had been moved to a place of safety, Jennings said politely, "Excuse me, Miss Thorpe, can you direct us to the paint-box department, please?"

"The – er —?" For a moment she was at a loss. Then her puzzled frown cleared and she said, "Well, I'm afraid we haven't got a special *department* for that sort of thing, but you could have a look on the twenty-pence oddment stall and see if there's anything there you like."

"Twenty-pence oddments!" Darbishire was horrified. "Oh, but my paint-box is worth at least two pounds."

"Keep quiet about it then," Jennings hissed in his ear. "I've got to buy it back, don't forget, and I can't afford fancy prices."

Darbishire kept his fingers crossed as they followed Miss Thorpe to a table in a corner of the room on which were several cartons containing an assortment of unsold articles in the lowest price range.

It was clear that Miss Thorpe's last-minute efforts to obtain some more stock had been only too successful. Indeed, there had been such a surplus of unconsidered trifles that many of the things that Mr Wilkins had salvaged from the lost property cupboard had failed to find a purchaser.

At first, Darbishire couldn't see his paint-box anywhere, though he recognised a geometry set belonging to Rumbelow and a punctured football bladder that had once been owned by Bromwich. He frowned in disapproval. Old Sir had really got a nerve sending these things here without asking! How would Sir like it if . . . Then he saw his paint-box.

"There it is, Jen," he crowed, doing a little dance of relief. "Oh, goodo—it hasn't been sold after all!"

Jennings had seen it too. He handed Miss Thorpe twenty pence, picked up the unconsidered trifle and returned it to its owner.

"It's a pity we can't afford to buy some of these other blokes' things back too," Jennings said as he recognised other familiar articles on the stall. "There's one of Venables' mini-cars, look! There's Martin-Jones' ping-pong bat, and Temple's golf ball."

"Coo! He's been looking everywhere for that old golf ball. He'd go up the creek if he knew where it had got to." Darbishire's voice was shrill with indignation. "It's a mouldy old chizz! I like Old Wilkie's cheek!"

Miss Thorpe was looking puzzled, so Jennings hastened to explain.

"We were just saying that a lot of these things shouldn't be here at all, by rights. They're not really rumble – er – jumble. They're lost property: they belong to boys back at school."

This was disturbing news for Miss Thorpe. She tightened her lips and said, "But I understood from the master who brought them along – Mr – er . . . "

"Mr Wilkins," Jennings prompted.

"Yes, Mr Wilkins. He told me that none of these things was wanted any more."

Jennings' wan smile and shrug of resignation were meant to suggest that Miss Thorpe had a lot to learn about the hardships of boarding-school life. "Well, of course *he'd* say that. *He* didn't want them. He'd think nothing of giving people's stuff away without asking permish."

"Without asking *whom*?" Miss Thorpe was ignorant of schoolboy idiom. "You mean Permish wasn't consulted either?"

"No. Permish isn't a person. Permish is short for permission," Jennings explained.

"Oh, I see! So you're implying that we had no right to offer any of these articles for sale?"

"Well, not really. Take that paint-box for instance. We had to come all the way down here and buy it back, just because Mr Wilkins couldn't be bothered to find out who it belonged to."

Jennings was beginning to enjoy himself. It was not often that he found a sympathetic adult to listen to criticisms of his form master. He ran his eye over the stall for further examples of injustice. "*And* that penknife, *and* that mini-car, *and* that bicycle pump. It wouldn't surprise me if the owners aren't searching all over the school for them at this very moment."

Miss Thorpe was aghast at the revelation. Her perky bird-like demeanour drooped and she looked like a bedraggled sparrow that has over-stayed its time in the bird-bath.

"This is *most* disturbing. You put me in a *very* awkward position," she twittered uncertainly. "I had no notion. I thought they were all gifts, freely offered for the good of the cause. In fact, I can hardly believe one of your masters would do a thing like that *deliberately*."

Darbishire, too, was anxious to gain sympathy by posing as a patient martyr. "That's all right," he assured her. "Don't worry about us. We're hardened to it by now. Besides . . ." He wanted to be quite fair to Mr Wilkins . . . "Well, it isn't so much *deliberate*: it just sort of happens. You have to make allowances for masters, you know. They don't see things like ordinary human beings."

But Miss Thorpe was not willing to make allowances. "But this is disgraceful!" she cried in forthright tones. The bedraggled sparrow had gone and now she looked more like an angry mother thrush protecting her young from a marauding magpie. "I am appalled to think of a grown man treating the boys in his care in this high-handed manner, and riding rough-shod over their feelings."

Jennings and Darbishire listened with a warm glow of approval. Miss Thorpe had the right ideas! It was not often that they had the pleasure of hearing Mr Wilkins' character torn to shreds by one of his own age group.

But her next words shattered the warm glow and wiped the satisfied smile from their lips. "It simply isn't good enough! I shall go straight up to Linbury Court and lodge a complaint in the strongest possible terms."

Jennings caught his breath in dismay and Darbishire was so shaken that he clutched at the table for support.

At all costs Miss Thorpe must be dissuaded from carrying out her threat! It was one thing to accuse Mr Wilkins of callous behaviour when he was safely out of earshot, and quite another to justify their words in the headmaster's study with the object of their reproaches standing there listening in scandalised indignation.

Of *course* they had overstated their case! Of *course* they had painted the picture in the blackest colours to make a good story out of it. But that didn't mean that they wanted strangers butting in and making trouble on their behalf.

"No, no! Really you mustn't do that," Jennings protested. "Please don't go and complain, for goodness' sake."

"Why not? I've only got to report what you have just told me to the headmaster and . . . "

"No, honestly. We'd rather you didn't."

"Nonsense," she retorted. "You're just trying to be chivalrous to shield the high-handed behaviour of one of your masters. But it simply isn't good enough. It's the principle I object to."

"The principal? You mean the headmaster?" Jennings queried. "Oh, he's not so bad when you get to know him."

"No, no! Princi-*pul*, not princi-*pal*. Mr Wilkins' conduct shows a wanton disregard for the rights of private property."

Darbishire gulped slightly and said, "Yes, we know, but I shouldn't go up to school and tell him so, if I were you."

Boys were odd creatures, Miss Thorpe reflected. They had been treated unjustly and didn't even *want* anyone to put matters right. One thing, however, was certain. All the unsold lost property brought along to the sale by Mr Wilkins would have to be returned to the rightful owners. Failing that, she told them, she would feel it her duty to complain to the headmaster in person.

Jennings and Darbishire really had no choice. The only way to frustrate Miss Thorpe's well-meant interference was to offer to return the articles themselves.

There were too many odds and ends for the boys to carry single-handed, but Miss Thorpe had a ready answer to this problem. "I'll ask Mrs Arrowsmith to take them up to the school in her car when she's finished her tea," she said. "She has a large boot, so she can easily cope with the unconsidered trifles."

"Trifles?" Darbishire queried, scanning the contents of the table with a puzzled look. "But we're never allowed to put food in the lost property cupboard, so what . . . "

"No, no! Not the edible variety. Just a quotation: Shakespeare, you know."

"Oh, I see. Well, would you please ask her to leave them outside on the playground," Darbishire said, for an awkward complication had just occurred to him. "Better not ring the bell and disturb Mr Wilkins. He might – er – he might be busy."

Miss Thorpe went off in search of Mrs Arrowsmith and the boys took their leave. As soon as they were outside the hall Jennings heaved a sigh of relief.

"Phew! That was a near thing! It would have been frantic if she'd come up to school and started creating. I can just see Old Wilkie's face when she told him he'd been ill-treating us."

"And I can just hear what he'd have said afterwards when she'd gone!" Darbishire gave a little shudder.

"Honestly, Jen, you are a clodpoll. It was all your fault, going on like that about Sir."

"Well, I like that! It was *you* who sounded all pathetic! It was *you* who woffled about having to put up with it, and all that flannel."

Darbishire giggled at the recollection. "Yes, we did lay it on a bit thick, didn't we!"

Chapter 8

The Unconsidered Trifles

It was nearly dark when Jennings and Darbishire arrived back at school. But not too dark for them to miss a large pile of cardboard cartons stacked near the side door of the building. Mrs Arrowsmith had got there first!

One glance was enough to show that something had gone wrong with the arrangements. True, the unsold contents of the lost property cupboard were there: but in addition there were several boxes and bags crammed with ornaments, clothing and household oddments.

"Oh, my goodness!" Jennings gasped. "These things aren't ours. What on earth has she unloaded all this lot on us for?"

The explanation was simple. When asked if she would take some boxes of odds and ends to Linbury Court, Mrs Arrowsmith had not known which articles were wanted and which were not. The usual practice, after a jumble sale, was to put out for the dustman all the unsold junk for which there was no further use. In the circumstances it had seemed best to her to include everything of doubtful value and leave it to the recipients to make their own selection.

The boys gasped at the pile in dismay. They had been planning to return the identifiable lost property to its rightful owners and give the rest as presents to deserving friends. But Mrs Arrowsmith's generosity had made this impossible. Who, for instance, would want half a dozen chipped enamel saucepan lids? . . . What could they do with four perished hot-water bottles, two egg whisks and a teapot stand? . . . Which of their friends was in need of a mildewed horse-collar?

"I suppose we could give *some* of it away," Darbishire said doubtfully. He picked up a lady's hat decorated with imitation cherries and a drooping pink feather. "How about this for Matron? She might look all right in it." He dug deeper into the carton. "Here's a pair of old bedroom slippers that'd probably fit Mr Wilkins. And here's . . . "

"Never mind that now," Jennings interrupted. "The first thing to do is to get this stuff out of sight before anyone sees it. If Old Wilkie starts asking questions and finds out Miss What's-it has sent it all back because of what we said about him . . ."

"Yes, I know, but where are we going to put the beastly things?" Darbishire flapped his fingers helplessly. "We can't leave them here and the tea bell will be going any minute."

"Don't panic," said Jennings. "Just for the moment we'll put it . . . " He searched his mind for a temporary hiding place. "I know! We'll put it back in the lost property cupboard."

"What!" Darbishire was appalled at the suggestion.

"But we can't put it in there. It's just been emptied."

"OK: there'll be plenty of room then, won't there! It's only for tonight. I'll get up early tomorrow and dump it somewhere safer before breakfast."

The risk of discovery was slight, Jennings argued, for Wednesday evening was not normally a time when matters concerning lost property were dealt with. "I'll stay here on guard while you go and get some blokes to help us carry it," he went on. "And for goodness' sake find out where Old Wilkie is first. We can't do it if he's on the prowl."

A few moments later Darbishire returned accompanied by Venables, Bromwich and Martin-Jones whom he had pressed into service and sworn to secrecy. Mr Wilkins, it appeared, had gone out in his car and Mr Hind, who was on duty, was in the music room rehearsing an item for the concert. The coast was clear.

Venables was delighted to see his mini-car again, and Martin-Jones was quick to claim his ping-pong bat.

"You can have them back as a reward for helping to carry the stuff," Jennings told them as they made their way indoors with the first batch of boxes.

"I should definitely think we *can* have them back," Venables retorted. "They're our own property, aren't they!"

"I'm not actually sure *who* they belong to really. You see, Old Wilkie gave them to this Miss Thorpe person, and she gave them to Darbi and me, so they're probably ours now, by rights."

"*Yours*! Well, I like the cheek of that! You give

me my mini-car back, or there'll be some bashing up going on around these parts."

"All right, all right! We can afford to be generous. You can have the horse-collar too, if you want it."

Without wasting any more time the five boys carried the jumble upstairs and started packing it in the lost property cupboard.

Darbishire put his paint-box on a nearby window-sill where he could keep an eye on it while he worked. He wasn't going to let his most favourite private possession get mixed up with the rubbish a second time, he told himself!

To begin with, they tried to arrange the jumble in some semblance of order, but this proved impossible when the bottom dropped out of two of the cartons, scattering the contents in an untidy heap.

The task was only half completed when the tea bell rang.

"Just another half-minute," Jennings urged. "We can't leave it like this."

"Yes, but what if . . . "

"Just bung it in anywhere. Don't bother to sort it out."

In frantic haste the boys crammed the odds and ends on to the shelves, the bulky objects on top resting on smaller ones beneath and only held in place by the pressure of still more objects being forced in from the front.

"We'll never get the door shut!" Darbishire moaned. "Look at that top shelf. Everything's all hanging out over the edge."

"It'll be all right." Jennings squeezed the last

object inside. "Now all shove together. One, two, three—push."

Somehow or other the door was forced shut on its protesting hinges and the latch slipped into place. Then, the five boys turned and scampered off to the dining-hall just in time to take their places for tea.

Mr Wilkins arrived back in his car as the boys were finishing the meal. He made his way upstairs just ahead of the throng leaving the dining-hall, and was about to go to his room when he noticed on the window-sill a paint-box with a blob of red sealing-wax on the lid.

Mr Wilkins frowned. Untidy little boys leaving things about after all the warnings he'd given them! They needed to be taught a lesson! He picked up the paint-box and turned towards the lost property cupboard across the corridor.

As he did so, a gasp of dismay sounded behind him. Looking round, he saw Jennings and Darbishire bearing down on him with expressions of deep concern on their faces.

"Sir! Sir! That's my paint-box you've got there, sir. May I have it back please?" Darbishire skidded to a halt and stood looking up at Mr Wilkins like a poodle hoping for a biscuit. "I left it there by mistake during tea, sir."

"Did you indeed! Well, I don't think you *can* have it back – at least not this evening," Mr Wilkins said in firm but kindly tones. "I shall confiscate it until this time tomorrow as a punishment for leaving it about."

"Oh, but sir!" The note of panic in Darbishire's voice was unmistakable.

"It'll be quite safe. I'm not going to eat it," Mr Wilkins assured him. "I shall merely put it away in the . . . "

"Oh, no, sir! Not in there!" Jennings broke in with the same note of urgency in his voice.

Mr Wilkins looked at him in sudden suspicion. "And why not, may I ask? I'm not accustomed to being told what to do, and what not to do, by boys in Form Three."

As he spoke he opened the cupboard door . . . and for the second time in less than a week leaped nimbly out of range as the cupboard spilled forth its treasures like a tipper-tuck unloading rubble on a building site.

But this time there was more – far more!

Mr Wilkins stared at the landslide with eyes that goggled with bewilderment. "*Doh!* Good heavens! How on earth . . . ! What in the name of thunder is all this stuff doing here!" he demanded in a bellow of exasperation. "I cleared this cupboard only last week. And now look! Rusty saucepans! . . . Women's hats! . . . Perishing rubber hot-water bottles!"

He glanced at the salvage collectors fidgeting from foot to foot with embarrassment. Their guilt was obvious from the expressions on their faces. "Did you put this rubbish in here?" he barked.

"Well, actually, yes, we did, sir," Jennings confessed. "But it isn't rubbish. You see, Mr Carter said we could go to the jumble sale and . . . "

"*Doh!* You must be off your heads, the pair of you. Do you think I went to all the trouble of emptying the cupboard so that you could fill it up again!" Mr Wilkins' eye fell upon a familiar pair of footwear. He picked them up and brandished them like a brace of life-preservers. "Oh, *no*! It's unbelievable! . . . *My* bedroom slippers!"

"Oh, are those yours, sir?" Darbishire inquired in surprise. "We were going to give them to you as a present."

Mr Wilkins performed a short Irish jig round the clutter at his feet. "But, you silly little boy, I threw them out because I wanted to get rid of them along with all this other stuff. And now, thanks to your stupidity, we've got ten times more lost property than we had before we gave it all away . . . What in the name of reason did you want to bring it all back for?"

Jennings looked at him in wide-eyed helplessness. "We didn't have any choice, sir. The lady said that if we didn't take it back she'd complain to the Head."

"Complain?" Mr Wilkins was baffled. "Complain about what?"

"About these things going to the jumble, sir." Jennings searched his mind for the exact words of Miss Thorpe's complaint. "She said – she said it simply wasn't good enough."

Mr Wilkins looked at him in surprise. "Well, that's a nice thing, I must say," he protested. "I provide her with all this stuff and she sends it back because it isn't good enough. It's the last time I'm going out of my way to do favours for the parish jumble sale, that's quite certain."

Jennings' conscience was about to suggest that that wasn't what Miss Thorpe had *really* meant, but

Mr Wilkins went on, "Well, it's not staying in here. Get some more boys to help you clear it all out of the way."

"Yes, sir. Where to, sir?"

"Don't ask me. It's all useless junk! Burn it, bury it, throw it away!"

More than half a dozen boys from Form Three volunteered to help with the removal. Under Jennings' direction they carried the contents of the cupboard across the playing-field and deposited them in the potting-shed near the headmaster's garden. Jennings was determined to keep the "unconsidered trifles" in safe keeping until he could dispose of them. To him it was unthinkable that they should be put out for the dustman. Given time, he was sure that he could put them to good use.

When the last of the jumble had been moved, Mr Wilkins continued on his way. To reach his room he had to pass the dispensary where, through the open doorway, he saw Matron dosing Binns and Blotwell, the youngest boys in the school, with spoonfuls of unappetising cough mixture.

She called out as he went past. "Oh, there you are, Mr Wilkins! I've got a phone message for you. A lady called Miss Thorpe rang up while you were out."

"Oh, she did, did she!" Bristling with injured pride, Mr Wilkins came into the room. "Believe it or not, Matron, that woman had the effrontery to send back our donation to her wretched jumble sale simply because it wasn't good enough."

"Yes, that was the phrase she used on the phone,"

Matron replied. "But it wasn't the contributions she was talking about: it was what she called your high-handed treatment of the boys. She considers you rode rough-shod over their feelings."

Mr Wilkins stared at her in amazement. "High-handed? . . . Rough-shod? . . . *Me*! What on earth does the woman mean?"

"She said it was most unfair that the things you sent her had been ruthlessly snatched from the hands of the defenceless owners." Matron smiled. "Her very words, if I remember right!"

"She must be mad!" Mr Wilkins' look of outraged indignation sent Binns and Blotwell into suppressed giggles of glee. "Whatever put an idea like that into her head?"

Matron turned away to replace the cork in the medicine bottle. She, too, seemed to be having some difficulty in keeping her features under control. "I've no idea," she replied. "Apparently she met two of our boys at the sale, so it's possible that some chance remark . . . "

"Jennings, of course! . . . And Darbishire, too! So *that's* the cock-and-bull story they told her."

Mr Wilkins' complexion turned a shade pinker. His eyes opened wide and he drew in his breath sharply, as though he had bitten an unexpectedly hot potato. Then he strode out through the door and shot an angry glance back along the corridor . . . But the lost property cupboard was deserted and there was no trace of the culprits to be seen.

"*Doh*! Just wait till I see those boys! I'll give them high-handed treatment! . . . I'll give them rough-shod riding! . . . I'll give them what simply isn't good enough! . . . "

He stormed away, still grumbling, to his room on the floor above and his wrathful complaints came wafting back through the open door of the dispensary. "The corridor knee-deep in tangled wreckage! . . . Egg whisks! . . . Horse-collars! . . . *My* bedroom slippers! . . . And they had the audacity to complain . . . "

His voice died away in the distance; and Matron turned back into the room to see Binns and Blotwell doubled up with convulsions of mirth.

She did her best to keep a straight face. "Come along, off you go! You've had your medicine," she said.

The two smallest boys made for the door with tears of merriment coursing down their cheeks.

"Coo, Matron, that was funny," Blotwell observed in the doorway. "I wouldn't have missed seeing Sir's face, not even if I'd had to drink *six* doses of that ghastly cough mixture."

Binns nodded in agreement. "Hear, hear! Worth every drop!" he confirmed.

Chapter 9

The Wooden Horse

It would not be true to say that nothing sensational happened during the rest of the week, for events which seem commonplace when they occur, sometimes develop in unexpected directions as time goes by.

The departure of Mrs Cherry, the school's cook-housekeeper, was a case in point. She left on the Thursday afternoon to take up a new post in London.

Everyone was sorry to see her go, for she was an excellent cook, and the first result of her departure was a falling-off in the quality of the school meals. Until a replacement could be found (and this proved more difficult than Matron had imagined), the cooking was undertaken by Mrs Hackett, who came in daily from the village to help with the washing-up.

Mrs Hackett, though a first-rate washer of dishes, made no claim to being even a third-rate cook, and for two weeks while the headmaster wrote to domestic agencies and inserted advertisements in the local newspaper, the school survived on a diet consisting mainly of tinned meat, boiled beetroot, and potatoes with hard centres.

Even so, no one could have forseen at the time the chain of events which led to the discovery of a reliable successor to Mrs Cherry. The events caused a crisis in the smooth running of the school routine, and when the disturbance came it was Jennings, of course, who was to blame – and also to be commended.

In the meantime Jennings had other things to worry about, and the chief of these was his failure to make the grade as a ventriloquist.

The trouble started in the classroom just before afternoon school on Monday. Under cover of his stamp album he was again studying the chapter on ventriloquism in his hobbies book, when Martin-Jones' shrill voice announced to all within earshot that the postman was coming up the drive.

Jennings looked up from his reading. He had a particular reason for being on hand when the parcel post arrived. Leaving the book on his desk, he hurried down to the front hall and was delighted to find a package awaiting him. The manageress of the Express Dry Cleaning Co had not let him down.

Matron was having tea in the dining-hall, so the coast to the dormitory was clear. Jennings scuttled up the stairs like a rat up a drainpipe and put his newly-cleaned shorts and sweater away on his shelf.

On his return to the classroom he found Venables at his desk, flicking through the pages of *The Bumper Book of Indoor Hobbies*.

Jennings was furious. He could have kicked himself for not hiding the volume before leaving the room.

"Hey! Give me that book. It's private!" he cried.

Venables crowed in triumph. "Aha! I told you I'd discover your famous deadly secret, didn't I?" Raising his voice and flourishing the book he addressed the room at large. "Listen, everybody! Fabulous news bulletin. Allow me to present J. C. T. Jennings, the world-famous ventriloquist – so he thinks. You can see the bits he's been learning by his dirty great fingerprints plastered all over the pages."

"You needn't have told everybody," Jennings retorted. "It was going to be a surprise item for the concert; and you've gone and spoilt it."

Temple and Atkinson abandoned their game of noughts and crosses on the blackboard in order to join in the argument.

"I bet you aren't *really* going to do it at the concert. I bet you can't do it at all, really," said Temple.

"Of course he can't. He's just swanking," said Atkinson.

"No, I'm not!" Jennings turned to his friend for confirmation. "I've been practising, haven't I, Darbi!"

Darbishire looked a little doubtful. "Well, yes, but I wouldn't say you're absolutely perfect yet. I can't tell the difference between the bluebottle and the man sawing wood. They both sound the same to me."

Jennings was hurt by this criticism from one who had promised his encouragement and support. "You're all against me – even you, Darbi! You wait till the concert, then. I'll show you! I'm going to borrow Blotwell's glove-puppet to use as a dummy and I'm going to . . . "

"Blah, blah, blah! Hark at old Big-head! It's always a lot of talk about what you're *going* to do – never what you can do now," Venables interrupted. "I bet you find some excuse to back out before the concert. If you're so marvellous, give us a demonstration."

"I *can* do it," Jennings persisted rashly. "It's just that I'm not feeling in the mood at the moment."

Venables, Temple and Atkinson hooted with derisive laughter. "I told you he'd back out of it!"

"Never heard such a feeble excuse!"

"Not in the mood! Tut! Do me a favour!"

The would-be ventriloquist scowled at the disbelievers. Honour was at stake! If he climbed down now he would never hear the last of it. Impulsively he blurted out, "All right, then! I'll give you a demonstration after tea."

"Why not now?" Venables wanted to know.

"Because – because there isn't time before school."

As though in support of this statement the bell rang and the group broke up and went to their desks to get ready for Mr Carter's English lesson.

Darbishire was gravely perturbed. "You must be off your rocker, Jen," he whispered to his friend as they sat down in adjacent desks. "You're not nearly good enough yet. Why on earth did you say you'd give a demonstration – and in front of witnesses, too."

"What else could I do?" Jennings defended himself. "They were all taking the mickey and I definitely wasn't going to let them get away with it."

"Yes, but what's going to happen when . . . ?"

"I don't know. I'll have to think of something."

Jennings heard very little of Mr Carter's English

lesson, for his mind was busy with the problem which he had so rashly undertaken. Though he hated to admit it, he knew deep down inside himself that he had no real hope of achieving his ambition in time for the concert a fortnight hence – let alone in time for a demonstration after tea! Surely there must be some way out of the dilemma!

By the end of the second lesson he had decided what to do. It wasn't a very practical plan: in fact, it was so bristling with snags that only sheer desperation forced him to work out the details.

He would hold the demonstration on the stage in the gymnasium, he decided, and make sure that the audience was a safe distance away in the body of the hall. On the stage he would place the vaulting-horse; and inside the vaulting-horse he would hide a confederate ready to supply the distant voice on which the success of the experiment depended.

Admittedly, the performance would be a trick, but he felt justified in practising a mild deception on an unfeeling audience whose only purpose in attending was to humiliate the performer and make him look foolish.

There was never any doubt about the choice of the confederate. After all, good old Darbi had long ago agreed to be his assistant and had pledged the contract with the secret thumb-pressing sign which must never be revoked. Very well then, here was his chance to play an active part in the entertainment. He ought to be grateful!

As soon as school was over, Jennings took his partner down to the tuck-box room to explain the plan he had in mind. Oddly enough, the assistant did not seem to appreciate the honour that was being accorded him.

"*Me*! Hide in the horse!" he cried in horrified dismay.

"Why not? It's hollow. You've only got to lift the padded bit off the top and climb in. You can even breathe inside: there's masses of knot holes."

"Thanks very much. Generous of you to let me breathe." Darbishire's tone was scornful. "You're crazy, Jen. They'd see through a dodge like that easily."

"Not if we're careful. I shan't let them get too close," the ventriloquist urged. "You see, I shall announce that I'm going to talk to a little man who's got shut inside. So naturally the audience will think it's really empty."

"Why should they think it's empty if you tell them there's someone in there?"

Jennings clicked his teeth with impatience. Really, old Darbi could be amazingly thick-headed at times.

"I shan't expect them to *believe* that. When they hear a squeaky voice coming out of it they're supposed to think it's me," Jennings explained. "Or rather, as they don't know about you, they'll think it's me making them think there's someone *else* in there."

"What – two of us?"

"No, you clodpoll – an *imaginary* person. Honestly, Darbi, you're not even *trying* to be helpful."

The assistant heaved a sigh of resignation. "I still don't see how it works," he objected. "You tell the audience there's someone in the vaulting-horse, and they don't believe you. And then afterwards you tell them it was just an imaginary person after all, so they definitely know they were right all the time. Is that what you mean?"

By this time Jennings himself was feeling confused. Darbishire's role was perfectly simple, he argued. All he had to do was to hurry into the gym after tea before anyone else arrived, and conceal himself according to instructions. He would have to stay in his hide-out until the demonstration was over and the audience had left, but that, surely, was no great hardship.

There was just one other detail which they had not yet settled. To ensure a successful performance, a short conversation of witty back-chat would have to be exchanged between the ventriloquist and the imaginary person in the vaulting-horse. A few lines of brilliant dialogue, sparkling with side-splitting jokes, would break down the atmosphere of doubt and convince the sceptics that their suspicions had been unjust.

Jennings had retrieved *The Bumper Book of Indoor Hobbies* from Venables before school, and now he turned hopefully to a passage at the back containing patter and gags for use during a performance.

"How about this, then," he said, and quoted aloud:

"Dummy: *A funny thing happened to me on the way to the theatre tonight. I saw a man with a flock of cows.*

Ventriloquist: *(correcting him) HERD of cows.*

Dummy: *Of course I've heard of cows. Big animals with a leg at each corner and racing handlebars on their heads."*

"Sounds a bit feeble to me," the assistant complained. "Besides, I've heard that ancient old joke before."

"Maybe *you* have. That doesn't mean to say that everybody else has. They'll probably think it's creasingly funny," Jennings replied. He ran his eye down the page. "It gets a bit better as it goes on. Listen:

"Dummy: *And one of these cows ran away, so the cow-master started shouting.*
Ventriloquist: *You mean the cow-herd.*
Dummy: *Oh yes, she heard all right. He was yelling his head off."*

They rehearsed the scene for five minutes by which time they were more or less word-perfect. Then they decided to pay a quick visit to the gymnasium before tea to put the vaulting-horse in position on the stage.

As they hurried off they saw Venables in the passage outside the tuck-box room, threading new laces into his football boots. He gave them a knowing smile and bent low over his work as they trotted past.

It was now four days since Mrs Cherry had left, and for the fourth day in succession the menu for tea had consisted of corned beef and half-baked potatoes.

"Oh, no! Not *again*!" groaned Atkinson as the boys went into the dining-hall for the evening meal.

"Mouldy chizz, mouldy potatoes," groaned Bromwich. "If this goes on much longer, I shall soon start *looking* like a baked potato."

"Nothing new about that. You've reminded me

of one for years," said Temple. He picked up the jacketed potato from his plate, squeezed it and shook his head sadly. "Bullet-proof!" was his verdict. "You'd never knock a nail through that with an ordinary hammer. You'd need a pile-driver." He glanced along the table for further proof of Mrs Hackett's shortcomings as a cook. "And just look at the tea! It's so weak it can hardly crawl out of the urn."

As a rule, Jennings was one of the most outspoken critics of school meals which fell below the usual standard, but on this occasion he was so concerned about his forthcoming demonstration that he hardly noticed what he was eating. He took little part in the chatter going on about him, and only once did the conversation of his colleagues register on his preoccupied mind.

This was when Venables, seated across the table, turned to his neighbour and said, "I say, have you heard that joke about the bloke who said he'd seen a flock of cows and his friend said, 'Herd of cows,' and he said . . . "

Jennings stiffened, and his half-baked potato dropped from his fork with a thud that set the plate dancing on the table-top. Surely Venables hadn't overheard the conspiracy being hatched in the tuck-box room!

If so, then all was lost and he might just as well . . . Then he breathed again, remembering that Venables had been reading *The Bumper Book of Indoor Hobbies* in the classroom before school . . . That, obviously, was where he had picked up the joke! Reassured, Jennings turned his attention again to his half-baked potato.

Darbishire was the first to leave the dining-hall as soon as the meal was over. With luck he would have about five minutes' start over the audience and that should be time enough to conceal himself in his hiding-place.

He was just crossing the hall when the staff-room door swung open and Mr Wilkins appeared on the threshold.

"Come here, Darbishire, I've got a job for you," he said.

The assistant ventriloquist blinked at him in dismay. "Oh, but, sir, I can't, sir. Now now. I've got a very important appointment."

"*How* important? With the headmaster? With the Prime Minister? With the Archbishop of Canterbury?"

"No, sir. With Jennings, sir."

"Exactly! And I'm not having you boys shirking your responsibilities just so that you can waste your time playing footling games."

"It's not a game, sir. It's terribly urgent. You see, he's going to talk to an imaginary little person inside the horse, so there's got to be a sort of squeaky voice coming out of it to answer him."

"Don't try to be funny, you insolent little boy," Mr Wilkins said sharply. "When I give an order I don't expect impudent answers about people being swallowed by horses with high-pitched voices. They're short-handed in the kitchen and I want some of you boys to help with the drying-up. Off you go!"

"But, sir . . . "

Mr Wilkins flung out his arm and roared in a voice that would have done credit to Henry V encouraging his troops at the siege of Harfleur. "To the kitchen!" he cried. "At once, boy, at once!"

Five minutes later a nervous ventriloquist ushered a critical audience of half a dozen boys into the gymnasium.

"You lot stand in the middle by the wall-bars," he said as he switched on the lights. And then, in sudden alarm: "Get off the stage, Venables! Only *I'm* allowed up there. Fossilised fish-hooks, who's giving this demonstration – you or me?"

Venables retired with bad grace and Jennings took his place on the platform. He began to feel more confident. The vaulting-horse was just as he had left it before tea, the only difference being that – according to plan – an unseen assistant should now be crouching inside awaiting his cue. It was a neat touch of old Darbi's to have climbed inside in the dark, he thought, for a room with the lights already on might well have raised suspicions in the minds of the audience.

Jennings's turned to the front, cleared his throat and said: "Ladies and Gentlemen! Sorry, I mean gentlemen only. First of all I am going to give a demonstration of what is known as the distant voice. I want you to imagine there's an imaginary person – er – let's see now, where shall we pretend he is?"

"Up in the roof," suggested Atkinson.

"No, not there," Jennings replied hurriedly. "Let's pretend he's accidentally got shut inside the vaulting-horse which you see behind me." He paused and favoured them with a winning smile. "Of course, as you all know, there's no one in there *really*, but . . . "

"Oh, yes there is!" shouted a voice from the audience. "And what's more, I'll tell you who it is. It's Darbishire."

Venables' outburst caused consternation. Eyes opened wide in protest as he went on, "I heard them planning it together in the tuck-box room before tea. You just watch and I'll prove it."

So saying, he marched up on to the stage followed by the entire audience and grabbed hold of the padded cover of the vaulting-horse.

"Get back! Keep off. You're spoiling my act," Jennings protested.

"We've got a right to inspect it, if we want to."

"No, you haven't. How do you think I can do my demonstration with you butting in like this?"

By now the entire audience was solidly in support of the interrupter.

"You daren't let us look because you know perfectly well old Darbi's in there," squawked Atkinson.

"That's right. I dare you to open it up. I challenge you!" bawled Temple.

Jennings jumped on the vaulting horse and sat astride. "Go away, all of you. It isn't fair," he shouted. "You've got to let me do it my own way."

His protests were ignored. Hostile hands grasped his legs while others dislodged his clutching fingers. A sharp push and he rolled from his perch and landed heavily on the floor.

"*Now* we'll see!" Venables chortled in glee. "Gather round, everybody, for ye famous revelation."

"Go away all of you. It isn't fair," Jennings shouted.

He lifted the padded lid from the horse and peered inside. At once his expression changed, and he stared down into the gloomy interior with a frown of surprise. "That's funny. He's not here . . . It's empty."

Temple pushed him out of the way to verify the facts for himself.

"Not a whisker!" he confirmed, and turned to Jennings with a grin of apology. "Sorry we roughed you up. Just like old Venables to get hold of the wrong end of the stick, as usual."

The ventriloquist rose to his feet and brushed the dust from his sweater. Of all the people in the room he was the most mystified at finding the vaulting-horse empty. Darbishire's disappearance had certainly eased a tricky situation, but what on earth had become of him?

Not by the flicker of an eyelid did Jennings betray his feelings of puzzled wonder. Instead, he strolled across the stage with a casual air and said, "I can't think what you were all making such a fuss about. I *told* you it was empty, didn't I!"

Bromwich turned to Martin-Jones and said,"That's right. He *did*, you know. Perhaps he really *is* a ventriloquist after all."

"OK, now's his chance to prove it," Martin-Jones replied. "Now we know there's no hanky-panky going on, he can get cracking with the famous act."

All eyes turned expectantly to the self-styled entertainer. But by now Jennings had shot his bolt. His confidence ebbed away, and when at last he spoke he was so overcome with confusion that he hardly knew what he was saying.

"Er – well, I will now give an impersonation of

a bluebottle sawing logs – er – I mean a bluebottle making a forced landing on the gred and gutter – or rather . . . " He tailed off into silence. It was hopeless. He knew he couldn't go on.

Once again it was Darbishire who saved the situation. For at that moment he came hurrying hot-foot into the gymnasium with an important announcement.

"Hey, you lot, break it up! Old Wilkie says you've got to go and help with the drying-up straight away," he declared. "I shouldn't keep him waiting, either. He's in a bit of a bate."

All this was perfectly true. The only point Darbishire failed to mention was that it was he himself who had suggested to the master on duty that he should go and recruit some more volunteers for the task on hand . . . Not that any extra help in the kitchen was really needed, but it was the only plan he could think of for helping his friend out of a very awkward predicament.

Jennings was quick on his cue. "Come on then, mustn't keep Sir waiting, must we!" He was through the door and halfway along the passage before anyone had time to register a protest.

In the dormitory that evening Jennings announced an alteration in the item he had planned for the concert.

"I've been thinking it over, and I've decided not to do my ventriloquism after all," he told Venables as they waited their turn at the wash-basins. "You see, there's a chapter on conjuring in that hobbies book, so I thought if I learned how to make someone *really* disappear from inside the horse – say, through a trap-door or something . . . "

"Oh, no!" An agonised protest came from the next wash-basin where Darbishire was foaming at the mouth with pink toothpaste. "We don't want any more capers of that sort, thanks very much."

"Why not? *The Mystery of the Vanishing Body*. Sounds a good trick to me," said Venables.

"Oh, it'd be a good *trick* all right," Darbishire conceded. "I'm thinking about the poor old vanishing body who gets dropped through the trap-door into a lot of inky blackness down below." He waved his tooth-brush in Venables' face to underline the importance of his remarks. "Because I can tell you here and now who old Jennings would pick for *that* little job . . . *Me*! Yours truly, C. E. J. Darbishire, in person! I can see it coming!"

Chapter 10

Vanishing Trick

Mr Hind eyed the cold sardines on his breakfast plate with distaste. "Oh for some bacon and eggs!" he exclaimed. "Oh for some fried sausage and tomatoes! Oh for a hot dish of almost *anything*." He shot a despairing glance at Matron across the table. "Any sign of a new cook on the horizon yet?"

She shook her head. "We've tried everywhere. The headmaster's advertising in the local paper again this week, but I'm not too hopeful. We didn't get any replies at all last time."

"Meanwhile, I suppose, we go on tightening our belts," observed Mr Wilkins who was sitting beside her. He took a drink of the muddy-coloured liquid in his cup and pulled a long face. "What's it meant to be this morning? Tea, cocoa, or cricket bat oil?"

"Instant coffee," she informed him.

"H'm! Instant death would be nearer the mark."

Matron smiled indulgently. "You must make allowances. Mrs Hackett does her best, but she doesn't profess to be a cook."

"That I can well believe," Mr Wilkins retorted with

deep feeling. "The boys are complaining bitterly. At tea yesterday, I found Martin-Jones eating boiled beetroot with his eyes shut. He said that if he couldn't see it, it was easier to pretend it was roast chicken."

The problem of finding an experienced cook to take Mrs Cherry's place was proving a more difficult task than had been supposed. Catering was not really Matron's responsibility, for she had more than enough to do in looking after the health and welfare of the boys: but in the absence of a cook-housekeeper she found herself becoming more and more involved in the domestic crisis as the days went by.

When breakfast was over she went to the kitchen for the daily conference about the menu. For some time Mrs Hackett had been growing resentful about the duties thrust upon her, and now she delivered her ultimatum.

"I'm only doing it to oblige, as I've told you before, Matron," she said firmly. "Washing-up's my job – not cooking for seventy-nine boys and a lot of grown-ups as well."

"Yes, of course, I do understand," Matron sympathised.

"I should hope so: and if something isn't done about it soon, I shall chuck in my hand. That's what I shall do, Matron – chuck in my hand."

Mrs Connie Hackett was a stoutish, middle-aged native of Linbury who was normally of an easy-going disposition. Her chief interest in domestic work lay in those jobs which could be tackled with slapdash vigour rather than skill. Indeed, such was the energy with which she set about the washing-up, that forks clattered on to the draining board with bent prongs, and plastic beakers crumpled under her heavy-handed grip. When she scrubbed the kitchen floor, she was so lavish with the contents of her bucket that the room took on the appearance of a children's paddling pool.

Matron did her best to soothe the ruffled feelings of the unwilling volunteer.

"I do appreciate all you're doing, Mrs Hackett, and as soon as we can find someone to take over I'll see you're relieved of the cooking," she said. "You don't know anyone from the village who'd do it, I suppose?"

Mrs Hackett's face puckered in deep concentration. "Let me have a think now!" There was silence while she coped with the problem. Then she said, "What you really want is an experienced cook like my friend Mrs Tebbut. Prepare a banquet fit for a king, she could."

"Really!" Matron's heart filled with rising hope. "Do you think we could persuade her to take the job?"

"Oh no! She's been dead five years, come Pancake Day."

"Oh!" The rising hope tottered, sank back and died quietly. "We'll just have to do the best we can then, and if you *would* be so kind as to carry on in the meantime . . . " Matron left the sentence unfinished. There was nothing to be gained by pointing out that boys and masters alike were all complaining about the monotony of cold meals. In her present mood, Mrs Hackett would probably have given notice on the spot.

"Well, all right then, Matron," the temporary cook said grudgingly. "But it'll have to be corned beef and potatoes again, that's all. And if you don't find someone to take over soon, I shall chuck in my hand. It's getting more than flesh and blood can stand, you know. After all, I'm only human!"

"Yes, of course, Mrs Hackett, I hadn't lost sight of that." Indeed it would have been impossible to forget that Mrs Hackett was only human, Matron thought, as she watched her preparing to wash up in her usual heavy-handed manner . . . No mechanical dishwasher would ever have tackled the task with so much noise and so much needless energy.

Now that the end of term was approaching, rehearsals for the concert took up a great deal of the performers' free time. The choir practised each evening after prep, the recorder players rehearsed in squeaky groups after breakfast, and solo pianists and singers suffered nervous attacks of internal butterflies at odd moments throughout the day.

Any room containing a piano was in demand during out-of-school hours, and as Mr Carter strolled around the building on his tour of duty on Tuesday evening, his ear was attacked by strange sounds wafting out from the music room on the second floor landing.

Mr Carter winced. He had a keen appreciation of music, and after listening for some agonising moments he thrust open the door, anxious to know what combination of instruments could contrive to sound like a steam-shovel scooping up dustbin lids.

Inside, Rumbelow and Atkinson were rehearsing their piano–and–violin duet, while Temple was squatting on the wastepaper basket cutting an india-rubber into small pieces to make himself a pair of ear-plugs.

"Hello, sir, isn't it chronic!" the maker of ear-plugs greeted him as the music screeched to a stop. "They're supposed to be playing 'The Fairies' Lullaby'." He mimicked the pianist's hand movements on the window-sill with grotesque gestures. "Crash, bam, wallop, wallop, wham, bang, crash! I shouldn't think anyone would get much sleep with that racket going on – least of all the fairies."

The musicians ignored the insult. "We're getting on quite well really," Atkinson observed. "It doesn't sound too bad, does it, sir?"

"Well, I have heard that piece played with a surer touch," Mr Carter was forced to admit. "*Must* you attack your violin as though it was a piece of scraperboard?"

"That's Rumbelow's fault, sir," the violinist defended himself. "He goes belting ahead on the piano like a bull on a bicycle without giving the poor old fiddle a chance to catch up."

"No, I don't. I slowed down to walking pace on that last bit and you were still half a mile behind," said the pianist. "Actually, I was going to wait for you at the bottom of the next page so we could both finish up together."

Mr Carter raised despairing eyes to the ceiling. "You'll have to do better than that or you'll have the audience walking out in the middle."

"Don't worry, sir. We've got nearly a week to get it up to Festival Hall standard," Atkinson assured him. "You will come to the concert, won't you, sir – you and Mr Wilkins and everybody?"

"Oh, yes, *do*, sir! It's my big chance to make my name in show business," urged Temple, whose sole function was to turn over the pages for the pianist. "I'll see everything's laid on for you, sir. Seats in the front row, clean programmes, ear-plugs, the lot!"

"Very kind of you," the master replied with a smile. "We'll be there all right. I'm sure Mr Wilkins won't want to miss hearing 'The Fairies' Lullaby' played as a rollicking hornpipe – especially when I tell him about the ear-plugs."

Downstairs in the tuck-box room another item was being prepared, and the performer was briefing his assistant in his duties.

Fortunately for Darbishire, Jennings had been obliged to abandon *The Mystery of the Vanishing Body* upon discovering that the gymnasium stage was not equipped with a trap-door. However, *The Bumper Book of Indoor Hobbies* had other suggestions to offer, and during the past two days he had given a great deal of thought to the selection of a suitable illusion.

"I've found two good tricks we *could* do, only one of them we'd better not because it means sawing a leg off a table and the Head might get a bit batey," Jennings informed his friend as he opened the book and turned to the relevant chapter. "The other one's all right though: it's a vanishing trick."

"Well, you can include me out, then," the assistant said firmly. "I'm not going to be shut up in a . . . "

"You don't have to be. It's not a person who disappears – it's a thing: like, say, somebody's gold watch. You stick it in an envelope and shake it about in a box till it turns up in someone else's pocket. Shut up talking, and I'll read you how to do it."

The method to be employed was easy to understand and the trick required no special apparatus apart from a card table covered by a cloth. It did, however, call for some skilful sleight of hand.

According to the instructions, the conjuror had first to conceal up his sleeve an object of the same shape and size as the borrowed watch, enclosed in a similar envelope. Then, under cover of by-play with a silk handkerchief and a magic wand, he had to substitute the hidden envelope for the genuine article, palming the latter into a pocket formed by pinning up one side of the cloth where it overlapped the table top.

When once the two envelopes had been exchanged, it was possible to have a great deal of fun at the expense of the horrified owner of the watch. His feelings at seeing what he mistakenly supposed to be his valuable property being ill-treated, rattled about in a box or even hit with a hammer, was guaranteed to cause the audience much heartless mirth.

Finally, by a further feat of dexterity, the original envelope with the watch safely inside had to be removed from its hiding place and slipped into the pocket of some unsuspecting member of the audience while the substitute was secretly disposed of in the folds of the tablecloth.

"Wow! Really crafty trick," Darbishire said admiringly. He had listened to the instructions with close attention, picturing the scene in his mind's eye. "It's just this business of swapping the envelopes over that sounds a bit dodgy to me. You don't want to make he same sort of bish that you did over that ventriloquist ark."

Jennings smiled knowingly: provided he could make ome small but vital alterations, he was confident of eing able to carry out the illusion with success. He ointed out that an experienced conjuror would invite ome unknown person to come up from the audience o assist him. He would have to exchange the envelopes ınder the eagle eye of this critical volunteer and plant he watch without his knowledge and consent. This vould be no mean feat and would call for the skill of a professional pickpocket.

But if, on the other hand, the "casual" helper vas really a confederate, the trick would be very nuch simpler to perform.

"That's where you come in, Darbi," the illusionist xplained. "When I ask for someone to come up, ou've got to make absolutely sure you get there irst."

"Great idea!" Darbishire approved, as the possiilities of the scheme took shape in his mind. "I ould, sort of, accidentally stand in the way so people ouldn't properly see what you were doing under the ilk handkerchief."

"That's right! And then I could – quite by chance – appen to be standing in front of you, so you could slip he watch into your pocket without anyone noticing."

"Yes, and I could look absolutely flabbergasted vhen it turned up in there at the end of the rick." Darbishire strode over to the mirror and ractised making faces to denote stunned amazenent and baffled wonder. Carried away, he made up a few lines of dialogue to heighten the effect. "Good heavens! Bless my soul! How ever did this get in my pocket! Astounding! Incredible! Who would have thought . . . "

"All right, all right, you don't have to recite the complete works of Shakespeare," Jennings said impatiently. "Let's have a bash at working out the details."

A quick visit to the common-room provided them with enough makeshift properties for their first rehearsal. Then, Jennings sealed a metal bottle top in one of the two envelopes he had collected and tucked it up his sleeve. The other envelope he placed on a table made of tuck-boxes, along with a toffee tin, a blackboard duster in place of a silk handkerchief and a school ruler for use as a magic wand.

"OK, I'm ready now, Darbi," he said. "You sit down and be a member of the audience."

"But you said I could be your assistant."

"So you can, only secretly. The audience have got to think that you don't know me."

"But that's crazy! Considering we've sat next to each other in class for the last . . . "

"I mean, they mustn't know you're connected with the trick." The conjuror picked up his magic wand and beamed at his imaginary audience on the tuck-box racks. "Good evening, ladies and gentlemen. Before I start my performance I shall require some disconnected person to come up and help me." He paused expectantly but there was no response. "Well, come on, Darbi – wake up! That's your cue."

"Oh, sorry! I was busy listening." The assistant

rose and came forward smirking self-consciously.

"I will now ask this unconnected person to go into the audience and borrow some rare article of genuine jewellery such as a priceless gold watch," the patter continued.

Darbishire glanced round and said: "Perhaps Old Wilkie will lend us his. He's got an ever so splendid one."

"Yes, OK," Jennings agreed. "After all, he couldn't very well refuse with everybody looking on, could he."

As a temporary measure, a coin was sealed in the spare envelope to represent Mr Wilkins' contribution to the feast of magic. There followed some furtive arm shaking under cover of the blackboard duster; and a little later the conjuror and his assistant met briefly in an awkward huddle like wrestlers seeking for a hold. But eventually the envelope with the coin inside was smuggled into Darbishire's pocket while its counterpart, containing the bottle top, lay on the table in full view of the imaginary audience.

"We'll have to practise that bit a lot more till we get it perfect," Jennings said, panting slightly from the exertions of the all-in wrestling. "Still, we'll press on with the rest of the trick and see how it works out."

This was the moment for some heavy-handed treatment of the disguised bottle top. Jennings threw the envelope into the toffee tin, slammed down the lid and rattled it as hard as he could.

Darbishire went weak at the knees with mirth. "Oh, fish-hooks, I can just picture Sir's face when he sees that and thinks it's his watch inside," he giggled.

"Poor Old Wilkie. He'll go into orbit and explode."

Jennings broke off his tin-rattling routine to say: "And we'll keep him guessing right up to the last minute, and then – *hey presto* – there's his watch safe and sound in your pocket. We ought to put this down on the programme as a rattling good trick." Delighted with his little joke, he roared with laughter and rattled the tin till it sounded like a hailstorm on the roof of a Dutch barn.

The noise attracted Mr Carter's attention as he made his way through the basement. Curious to know the cause of the commotion, he opened the door and stood looking at the cavorting conjurors with interest.

"Oh, hello, sir!" Darbishire welcomed him with obvious pleasure. "We're practising a trick for the concert. You'll never guess what it is!" He shot an uncertain glance at his friend. "Shall we tell him, Jen, or is it a secret?"

With an effort Jennings controlled his mirth and said, "Well, we shouldn't really, of course, but I can't resist telling you one bit, sir – it's too funny for words. Provided you promise not to spread it, that is."

Mr Carter's nod was as good as his word.

"Well, sir, we're going to borrow Mr Wilkins' watch and shake it like this," Jennings said, suiting the action to the word.

"H'm. You'll be popular!" was Mr Carter's verdict.

"You do think he'll lend it to us, don't you, sir?"

"How can you doubt it?" Mr Carter replied dryly,

as the dormitory bell shrilled out its bedtime message. "I'm sure nothing would give Mr Wilkins greater pleasure on the last night of a hectic term than to listen to his valuable watch being rattled to bits in a rusty toffee tin."

Chapter 11

Open Invitation

The problem of what to do with the jumble in the potting-shed was now becoming acute. Obviously, it would have to be disposed of before the headmaster discovered that a useful outbuilding had been converted into a depository for the unsold remnants of the village rummage sale.

So far the fact had escaped his attention, but this state of affairs could not be expected to continue for ever . . . Something would have to be done!

On Thursday afternoon just before football, Jennings and Darbishire paid a visit to the potting-shed. For a fortnight they had been putting off the question of how to cope with their unwelcome inheritance. Now, they decided to seek inspiration by taking another look at it.

Darbishire ferreted amongst the pile and picked up Temple's golf ball. "Well, here's one thing we can give back, anyway."

"Fat lot of help that is," Jennings said scathingly. "Ten million tons of stuff to get rid of, and you have to pick out a titchy little thing weighing 0.1 per cent of minus half an ounce."

"Well, it's a start. And Rumbelow can have his geometry set and Bromo can have his old bladder back. And for the other things we could – we could —" The scavenger dug down into the heap and produced an egg-cosy and a cut-glass cruet. "How about this as a hat for Blotwell's glove puppet? And Binns could keep his coloured inks in these little bottles. He could put red ink in the pepper pot and green ink in the mustard pot and . . . "

"Oh, for goodness' sake!" Jennings broke in impatiently. "We want to clear the whole lot in one big swoosh. We haven't got time to muck about making puppets' hats and wondering whether the purple ink will look all right in the salt-cellar. If we don't get this shed emptied before the weekend, somebody's going to start creating."

For some seconds Jennings stood frowning at the junk in deep thought. Then his eyes lit up as a bright idea skidded over the surface of his mind. "We'll have our own jumble sale, that's what!"

Darbishire looked at him in surprise. "You're bonkers! How could *we* have a jumble sale? We'd never get permish to hire the village hall for one thing and . . . "

"No, not in the village hall. Here, at school. A free jumble sale where all the blokes can pick what they want for themselves free of charge, and have the rest to take home as Christmas presents for their mothers and fathers and people."

Darbishire gazed at his friend in wide-eyed admiration. This was the perfect solution to their problem. The saucepan lids, the ornaments, the egg-whisks – all those objects which had promised to be so difficult to dispose of, would be snapped up at once if they were described as Christmas gifts for aunts and godmothers.

There was only one drawback to the scheme and Darbishire felt bound to point it out. "We'll have to get permish," he said. "So bags you do the asking."

"Yes, all right," Jennings agreed. "I'll ask Mr Carter when Old Wilkie's not about, and if he says it's OK we'll have it in the gym on Saturday."

"Great idea! We may need one or two blokes to help, but we shall be the ones in charge, shan't we? Just you and me, eh?"

Jennings nodded. "Of course. Joint-managers," he confirmed. "Let's have a pact of agreement on it." They pressed their thumbs together to seal the contract.

In the distance a referee's whistle shrilled out, signalling the start of their football practice.

"Hey, come on! Time we weren't here." Jennings slammed the shed door and led the way to the football pitch at full gallop.

Darbishire followed at a jog-trot. In his mind's eye he could already see the gymnasium transformed into a bustling department store crowded with carefree customers doing their Christmas shopping. In charge of the crowd were two courteous joint-managers handing out free gifts and wishing their customers the compliments of the season.

The whistle blew again, more urgently this time, and Darbishire broke into a run . . . Even courteous joint-managers of important supermarkets had to wake their ideas up when Mr Wilkins was refereeing the Form Three football game.

* * *

After tea that evening Jennings and Darbishire went to the staff-room in search of Mr Carter.

According to Venables, Mr Wilkins had been seen heading towards his garage at the end of afternoon school and might therefore be presumed to be safely off the premises.

"Much better to ask when he's out of the way," Jennings observed as they trotted along the corridor. "Mind you, he'll have to know about it some time, if Mr Carter says 'Yes,' but I'd rather not have him standing there kicking up a hoo-hah until we've got everything settled."

When they knocked at the door it was Mr Carter's voice that invited them to enter, but once inside the room they found that the senior master was not alone.

Venables had been wrong! Mr Wilkins was sitting reading the evening paper.

"And what can I do for you?" Mr Carter inquired.

Jennings hesitated, and then decided to go ahead with his request. After all, he reasoned, it was Mr Wilkins' fault that the things had been sent back from the parish hall in the first place – well, *partly* his fault, anyway.

"Well, sir, it's about the stuff that – er – that *used* to be in the lost property cupboard," he began. "Mr Wilkins told us to take it away so we put it in the potting-shed, just for the time being as you might say."

The evening paper rustled its pages in a menacing manner. "*I* never told you to put it in the potting-shed,"

Mr Wilkins denied brusquely. "I told you to get rid of it. I assumed you'd done so a couple of weeks ago."

"But, sir, there was nowhere to put it," Jennings explained. "We couldn't have a bonfire because of all the model railway lines and saucepans that wouldn't burn, and in any case we wanted to give some of the things back to the blokes who'd lost them."

Mr Carter intervened to say that there was little point in making excuses about what should have been done a fortnight before. If the matter hadn't been dealt with already, the sooner it was settled the better for all concerned.

"Yes, sir, that's what we've come to see you about," Jennings went on. "Will you very kindly give us permish to have a jumble sale?"

Mr Carter smiled, but his colleague wheeled round in his chair in scandalised protest.

"Jumble sale!" he echoed, as though Jennings had suggested a flight to the moon. "What on earth are you talking about? This is a school, not a Women's Institute. We don't *have* jumble sales!"

Jennings held his ground and looked Mr Wilkins in the eye. "Not ordinary ones, no, sir," he conceded. "But this one's rather special, you see. It's a jumble sale, free of charge."

"Tell me more," said Mr Carter.

"Well, sir, if you'll just give us permish, we're going to spread all the stuff out on the floor in the gym and let everybody claim their own things back and take anything else they want."

Mr Wilkins snorted. "Free jumble sale! Tut! Never heard such a fantastic idea." He turned back to his paper. "Still, it's up to you, Carter. I wash my hands of it."

In spite of his colleague's disapproval, Mr Carter did not condemn the idea out of hand. Indeed, it seemed to him a practical way of restoring a fair amount of lost property to its rightful owners.

"All right, then! You can have it in the gym," he agreed. "There isn't a match this Saturday so it'll be something to keep you out of mischief."

"Oh, thank you, sir. Thank you ever so much, sir."

The two joint-managers wasted no time. As soon as they left the staff-room they hurried off to appoint "free" salesmen to help with the project. Venables, Temple and Atkinson were chosen for this important task, and all accepted with enthusiasm. A short meeting was held just before evening prep at which the assistants were instructed in their duties.

"We'll lug the stuff over from the potting-shed and spread it all out in the gym at break on Saturday," Jennings told them. "We'll have different departments like say, for instance, *Gents' Millinery* or *Genuine old antique ironmongery*, and we'll each be in charge of one section, just like a proper supermarket."

"Bags I don't have those ghastly old women's hats," Temple protested. "I shan't get a single customer."

"I don't see why not. They'd be really useful as pen-wipers, or for keeping conkers in, or something," Darbishire suggested.

"We want everybody to come – masters as well," Jennings impressed upon his helpers. "I'll make out some posters and stick them up where everyone will see them. If they know there are going to be free presents for one and all, we're bound to get a good crowd."

"It'll be more like a Christmas bazaar than a jumble sale," Atkinson decided. "Perhaps we ought to stick little blobs of cotton-wool on the windows to look like falling snow, and paint some torch bulbs to look like fairy lights; and for a Christmas tree we could have . . . "

"No, we flipping well couldn't," the chief organiser interposed firmly. "We'll have quite enough to do sorting the stuff and dishing it out, without mucking about with little blobs of sticky cotton-wool all over the place. Just one or two high-class posters in good taste. That'll bring them flocking, you see if it doesn't."

Jennings never spoke a truer word! Though at the time, even *he* could not have foreseen the unexpected results of the tasteful publicity.

For the past few days, Jennings and Darbishire had spent the morning break in rehearsing their conjuring trick for the concert. Mr Hind, whom they had approached when his mind was on other matters, had granted them half-hearted permission to include the item on the programme, and they were determined not to forego this honour by being unprepared.

On Friday, however, they were obliged to cancel the rehearsal in favour of their latest project planned for the following day. So while Jennings went off to the art room in search of three large sheets of drawing paper, Darbishire borrowed a box of crayons so that the lettering on the posters should attract the eye by its colourful appeal.

The morning break was over by the time they had

collected their materials, but in the rest period after lunch the boys set about their task in earnest.

Jennings took a sheet of drawing paper from his desk and opened the box of crayons. Then, in letters of red, orange, yellow, green, blue, indigo and violet he spelt out the invitation:

Grand Jumble Sale
in the gym.
on Sat at 3 pm.
Fabulous Free Gifts for All!
Everybody Invited!!
Admission Free!!!

When the rest period was over Jennings pinned up one of his posters in the common-room and another in the library. The third one he decided to hang on the noticeboard in the entrance hall. All the boys and masters passed by that way several times a day and could hardly fail to observe a poster in such a prominent position.

Matron and Mrs Hackett were talking together in the hall when Jennings arrived. Having finished the midday washing-up, the temporary cook was preparing to go off duty for a couple of hours before returning to cope with the evening meal.

"It's no good, Matron! I've told you before," she was saying in tones of complaint, "if you can't find someone to take over by the end of the week I shall chuck in my hand."

"The end of the week! But that only gives us until tomorrow!" Matron was appalled at the prospect of having no-one at all to take charge in the kitchen. "I really don't know how we shall manage. We've got another advertisement in this week's local paper, but no-one has applied so far."

Mrs Hackett buttoned up her coat and pulled her beret well down over her ears. "Well, I'll be getting along now. Be back at me usual time for the boys' tea." She started to cross the hall and then stopped, her eye caught by the gaudy lettering on the noticeboard.

"What's this, then? Grand jumble sale, eh?" she queried.

Jennings was still in the hall admiring his handiwork from different vantage points. "Oh, it's just something we're going to have tomorrow," he said casually. "Should be rather good fun."

He didn't enlarge upon the subject as it never occurred to him that Mrs Hackett might be interested in what was, after all, a strictly private function.

"Fancy that now! Never had a jumble here before. Not in my time anyway." She nodded approvingly and walked on.

Mrs Connie Hackett went home for her two-hour break pondering the poster's message. She was an ardent supporter of parish jumble sales and never missed a visit to the village hall whenever there were bargains to be had for the snatching.

Fabulous Free Gifts For All, the poster had said . . . Fancy that now! Her neighbour, Mrs Clough, would be glad to hear about that. A great one for free gifts was Bertha Clough . . . *Admission Free*, too . . . That was nice! Her neighbour on the other side, Mrs Pinmill, would certainly thank her for *that* information. Always resented the twenty-pence entrance money, did Ethel Pinmill.

Everybody invited it said at the bottom . . . Well, that was as it should be! Quite a lot of her friends had never been inside the school. Never set foot in the place, even. Well, here was their chance! It was a good job she'd seen that poster, she thought. There was nothing like a good lively jumble sale to brighten up a winter's afternoon.

Mrs Hackett made her way down the village street stopping every so often to spread the tidings of this new and unexpected event in the rural calendar.

Unlike Jennings, it never for a moment occurred to her that a jumble sale could possibly be anything but a public event!

Chapter 12

The Lure of the Jumble

December 16th is remembered by historians as the anniversary of the Boston Tea Party, the occasion upon which a band of American colonists caused chaos by invading a ship in the city harbour. At Linbury Court the date is memorable as the anniversary of the Free Jumble Sale, the day when a band of bargain-hunters caused comparable chaos by invading the school premises.

At five minutes to three the following afternoon, Jennings and Darbishire stood in the middle of the gymnasium looking about them with a contented air. They and their assistants had worked well. During morning break they had carried the stock from the potting-shed and spread it out on the gymnasium floor.

Judged by parish hall standards the collection was meagre and practically worthless, but the two joint-managers seemed more than satisfied with the goods they had to offer.

For example, the toy department had an excellent range of mini-cars (with wheels and without), slightly dented ping-pong balls and jigsaw puzzles ɹith only a third of the pieces missing. The fancy oods department with its range of picture frames, ·ld gramophone records and babies' bootees was a .appy hunting ground for any nephew seeking a easonable free gift for a not-too-popular uncle or unt: while in the *Do-it-yourself* section, a hobbies nthusiast could find a number of things to convert ɔ his use – a flower-pot stand for a camera tripod, cracked saucer for target practice, a clock face for a paceship's instrument dial, a horse-collar for a – for – well, there must surely be *something* one could do ɹith a mildewed horse-collar, even if it meant seeking ·ut a shirehorse with an incomplete wardrobe.

Outside in the corridor Binns and Blotwell, first in he queue, pressed their noses to the glass panel of the .oor. Behind them a dozen boys had assembled, and ıore were arriving every minute.

And now all was ready. The two joint-managers ·ressed their thumbs together as an augury of good ıck.

Jennings glanced at the clock. "Five minutes to go nd then—" He picked up a watering can and sounded fanfare down the spout. "Da-da-da-*dah*! I declare ye amous jumble sale well and truly open."

Atkinson glanced out of the window and said, Hey! Who are all those old women over by the side .oor?"

Venables followed the direction of his friend's ·ointing finger. Across the playground at the extreme nd of the main building, a score of women carrying hopping bags were huddled together, deep in conver- ation.

Venables shrugged. "I don't know. What about them? They're nothing to do with us."

"No, I know. I just wondered who they were."

"Well, stop wondering and go and stand by your department ready to serve," Jennings commanded, dismissing the ladies outside with a glance of indifference. "You'll have plenty to do when we let the blokes in, without bothering about people holding Mothers' Meetings or whatever they've come for. It isn't our business anyway."

The gathering on the playground was observed by Mr Carter as he stood chatting to Matron on the first floor landing. Mildly curious, he asked, "Anyone expecting visitors? Or is it a weekend conference of some sort?"

"I've no idea," Matron replied, eyeing the group with vague interest. "Unless, of course—" She broke off. Her vague interest suddenly changed to wild hope, and she exclaimed, "Good heavens! How marvellous! But surely they couldn't *all* be cooks, could they!"

"Cooks?" For a moment Mr Carter was at a loss.

"That advertisement we put in today's local paper. I was hoping one or two might read it and come along, but this is better than anything I dared hope for."

It certainly seemed a remarkable response after two weeks without a single applicant, and Mr Carter shook his head doubtfully. "There must be a lot more unemployed cooks around these parts than anyone knew about, if your theory's right."

"Of course I'm right! There's nothing else they *could* have come for. What a stroke of luck!"

She must start interviewing the candidates at once,

she decided. There were so many of them that the task of choosing a successor to Mrs Cherry would take her the rest of the afternoon.

With a clatter of juvenile footwear, Bromwich and Rumbelow trotted into view, heading for the jumble sale in the gymnasium.

Matron hailed them with some urgency. "Come here, you two! I've a little job for you. Escort duty. If you go down to the side door you'll find some ladies waiting."

"Yes, Matron, we've seen them. We were wondering who they were," said Bromwich. "They look a bit old to be some blokes' mothers, or even some blokes' grandmothers. Of course, they could be some blokes' great-grandmothers or even . . . "

"Yes, but they're not. They've come to take Mrs Cherry's place as cook-housekeeper."

"What, *all* of them? But you'd never get all that lot in the kitchen at the same time, Matron."

Patiently she explained. "No, Bromwich, we only need one."

"Oh, I see! It'd be a case of too many cooks spoiling the broth otherwise, wouldn't it!" Bromwich went off into peals of mirth at what seemed to him was the wittiest retort of the year. "I say, that was really clever, wasn't it, Matron! Did you hear what I said? I said too many cooks spoil . . . "

"Yes, dear, very funny, ha-ha, but we mustn't keep them waiting," Matron said hurriedly. "Just ask them in, and show them the way up to my room. And mind you're very, very polite."

"Yes, Matron. Of course, Matron."

Bromwich and Rumbelow clattered away on their errand, the former repeating his joke for the third time in case the latter hadn't seen the point.

Mr Carter turned away from the window wearing a slightly puzzled look . . . All those shopping bags! Was it usual, he wondered, to take *quite* so many paper carriers, baskets and plastic containers when applying for a job? Still, Matron knew best and she seemed happy enough!

"Good luck then, Matron! I hope all goes well at the interviews." With a wan smile he added, "Who knows, we may yet enjoy a hot meal before the term is over!"

Still smiling, he went off to the staff room to mark Form Three's English books.

When the two escorts reached the ground floor, Rumbelow said, "All right, you needn't tell me *again*, Bromo. I laughed the first six times, but it's getting a bit stale now. Let's hurry up and let the old girls in so we can get off to the gym."

"What d'you mean, 'old girls'?" Bromwich was shocked. "Matron said we'd got to be very polite to them."

"OK, I'll practise on you." In exaggerated tones of mock politeness, Rumbelow twittered, "Good afternoon, Mrs Bromwich. I trust I find you in good health."

Bromwich took up his cue in accents so refined that speaking made his nose twitch like a rabbit's. "So kind of you to inquire, Mrs Rumbelow. Actually, my ingrowing chilblains have been bothering me something chronic, these cold nights."

By now they had reached the side door. Bromwich swung it open and then stood back in surprise as the first wave of invaders bore down on him like runners in a mass-start cross-country race jockeying for position.

First across the threshold was Mrs Bertha Clough, a large lady with a husky voice and a determined manner.

"About time someone let us in! Been waiting twenty-five minutes," she complained, and turned to a depressed-looking woman beside her wearing a pink plastic mac. "That's right, isn't it, Ethel?"

Mrs Pinmill (Ethel to her friends) confirmed the fact with a gloomy nod. "Didn't do my bad back any good waiting out there in the cold," she grumbled.

It was not necessary to invite the visitors to enter for they had already done so, and were now fidgeting with impatience to get to their destination.

Bromwich did his best to take control. "Good afternoon, ladies," he said loudly (and very politely). "If you will kindly follow me and this freckle-nosed bloke here, we'll take you up to Matron's room."

The group looked at him with mistrust. "Take us *where*?" queried a lady in a purple head-scarf.

"Up to see Matron. She's expecting you. About doing the cooking."

The ladies exchanged puzzled glances, and Mrs Clough said firmly, "We haven't come here to see no Matrons. It's the gym we're looking for."

"The gym! Oh, but you can't go in *there*," Bromwich protested. "There's a jumble sale going on. It's just about to start."

"That's right. Three o'clock, Saturday," the ladies confirmed, nodding to one another.

"Free gifts for all," added Mrs Pinmill. "That's what it said on the poster, according to Connie Hackett. We're friends of hers, see. She's going to join us as soon as she's finished in the kitchen."

"But it's a *private* jumble sale, just for the boys," Bromwich insisted. "It's not meant for the public at all."

Mrs Pinmill brushed the objection aside. "Connie Hackett never said anything about that. Everyone invited, she said. Admission free, and all."

There was a restless stirring among the group; brown paper carriers rustled impatiently and coins jingled in coat pockets. Seasoned jumble-sale customers were not going to have their plans thwarted by unhelpful small boys.

Mrs Clough, an obvious leader, took command. "What are we standing about arguing for?" she demanded. "No use wasting time with these lads, or it'll be all over before we get there."

So saying, she strode off down the corridor with her supporters pressing closely on her heels. When they reached the corner they found themselves in a rectangular hall with a staircase ahead and doors and passages leading off in other directions.

Mrs Clough gave the order to halt while they discussed their next move. Unfortunately, Mrs Hackett had been delayed in the kitchen, and without her to act as guide none of the party knew which way to go.

"Split up, shall we?" suggested the leader. "Ethel

and Doris and me up these stairs: Gladys and Mrs Lumley and some of you others try that passage on the left, and the rest go the other way through that green door."

The party divided up into groups, spread out fanwise, and set off on their tours of exploration.

"First one to find it call the others!" the leader shouted after them. "And look sharp about it. No point in coming all this way for a jumble if all the best bargains have gone before we find the way in."

As the party disappeared from view, the escorts, trailing along behind them, stopped and admitted defeat.

"There's nothing we can do about it if they won't even listen," Rumbelow observed with a shrug. "Better go and tell old Jen to stand by for a flood of extra customers, that's all."

Mr Carter had only just started to mark Form Three's essays when the staff room door burst open and a very harassed Mr Wilkins strode into the room.

"I say, Carter, just what *is* supposed to be happening?" he demanded.

"Happening? This afternoon?" Calm and unhurried as usual, Mr Carter looked up from his work. "Well, let me see now! There's football coaching for the first XI, the Head's taking a few boys into town in his car, the juniors are having their fun and games in the gym and . . . "

"No, no, no! I'm not talking about school routine," his colleague broke in irritably. "How you can sit there quietly marking books with a full-scale riot going on left, right and centre . . . "

"Really? Who's rioting?"

"Women! Hordes of them!" Mr Wilkins waved his arms in the air like semaphore flags. "The school's been invaded, swamped, overrun by a monstrous regiment of women charging about the building like a herd of buffalo, waving shopping bags and brandishing umbrellas."

"H'm! I doubt whether a buffalo would actually *brandish* an umbrella, or even . . . "

"Don't quibble, Carter. I tell you the situation is completely out of hand and something has got to be done!" Mr Wilkins thumped the table and went for a short walk round the room to relieve his feelings. "In the first place, who are these women and what are they doing here?"

"That's quite simple." Mr Carter drew a red circle round a misspelled word in Atkinson's exercise book. "I need hardly remind you that for the last fortnight none of us has had a decently cooked meal!"

"Yes, I know all about that, but . . . "

"That's the explanation. These ladies are prospective cooks who have come along in response to the Head's advertisement. At the moment they are on their way up to Matron's room to be interviewed for the vacant post."

"Oh, no, they're not!" There was no mistaking the firm note of conviction in Mr Wilkins' voice. "They've none of them gone anywhere *near* Matron's room. They've spread out like a battalion of infantry engaged in mopping-up operations and penetrated to every part of the building."

Mr Wilkins had reached the limits of his patience. On first encountering the ladies of Linbury, he had tried to ascertain the reason for their visit, only to find himself swept aside like a pocket of resistance in the path of a spearhead attack. His questions had gone unheeded, for Mrs Clough and her friends were far too busy to waste time in idle chat with some strange man they had happened to pass on the staircase.

The realisation that, as master-on-duty, his authority was being flouted and his orders ignored had upset Mr Wilkins very much indeed. Quivering with indignation, he cried, "You don't seem to understand, Carter! There are women in the classrooms, women in the library, women in the tuck-box room, women in the dining hall, women in the dormitories. Women *everywhere* – except in Matron's room!"

Mr Carter laid his marking aside and the two masters hurried out to investigate.

Although Mrs Clough was gifted with obvious powers of leadership, her plans for rallying her supporters in a frontal assault upon the gymnasium suffered from a certain lack of organisation.

Some of the women got lost in the basement and were unable to contact their leader. Others abandoned the idea of attending the sale in favour of a sightseeing tour of the building. Those whose feet were aching as a result of the half-mile walk from the village sank down with thankful sighs in the armchairs in the library and went no farther. A few who had brought sandwiches to sustain them, decided that a snack in comfortable surroundings was preferable to trapesing about corridors that seemed to lead nowhere.

Thus it was that when Mr Carter and Mr Wilkins started their investigations, the ladies of Linbury were widely dispersed in various parts of the building.

In the hall they were just in time to catch sight of the woman in the purple headscarf hurrying up the stairs. Mr Wilkins did his best to attract her attention. "I say, excuse me, Madam – er, Madam, I say! Just a minute! Do you mind . . . "

But his efforts were useless. Either she had omitted to switch on her hearing aid or she was out of earshot before he spoke, for she took no notice and disappeared in the direction of the library.

Mr Carter was puzzled. "What is it they're looking for?" he demanded.

His colleague shrugged helplessly. "I don't know. They're all so busy rushing about that you can't get a word of sense out of them."

In the distance he spied a woman in a green coat emerging from a classroom and heading for the kitchen quarters farther along the corridor. "Madam! Madam! Look here, I say, you can't . . . "

But she was through the door before he had finished his sentence.

"Don't worry," Mr Carter consoled him. "She can't do much harm in the kitchen. Mrs Hackett's baked potatoes are just about indestructible."

They were about to follow her when they saw Matron coming down the stairs. She appeared somewhat perplexed.

"What's happening?" she asked. "I've been waiting in my room all this time and not one of the applicants has come along to be interviewed."

"I'm not surprised. They haven't come here to do the cooking, that's quite certain," Mr Wilkins told her.

"Who are they, then?"

"We don't know."

The riddle was solved almost immediately by the appearance of Mrs Hackett, flanked on either side by Mrs Clough and Mrs Pinmill and other members of the social group, who came sweeping along the corridor at a brisk five miles an hour *en route* for the gymnasium.

Mrs Hackett beamed amiably. "Afternoon, Matron. Just a few of my friends from the village," she explained. "They've come along for the jumble."

"The what?"

"The jumble in the gym. We thought we'd make an outing of it, seeing as I'm free till washing-up time."

The significance of this remark was not lost on Matron. "But what about getting tea *ready*? Surely you're going to do that as well?"

Mrs Hackett pursed her lips and shook her head. "Sorry, Matron! Chucked in my hand, like I said." Her tone was firm, but kindly. "After all, I did warn you."

The ladies around her were seething with impatience to be on their way. "Come on then, Connie," urged Mrs Clough, nudging with her elbow. "It'll be over before we get there, else." Her eye ranged round her supporters. "Tut! Now we've lost Mrs Clutterbuck! Where's she got to?"

"It's all right, Bertha," Mrs Pinmill assured her. "She's having a nice sit-down with Mrs Lumley in that room with all the books."

"Have they got their sandwiches?"

"Oh, yes. They're quite comfortable."

An explosive sound like a football capsizing under pressure forced its way through Mr Wilkins' vocal chords as the ladies plodded off down the corridor behind Mrs Hackett.

"*Doh*! Picnics in the library!" he spluttered. "I never heard such a . . . Who in the name of thunder told Mrs Hackett she could invite all her friends here?"

What seemed more important to Matron was what she was going to do about the next meal. "This is hopeless," she lamented. "Now Mrs Hackett has put her foot down, there's absolutely no-one in the kitchen at all."

"That's not strictly true, I'm afraid," Mr Carter observed, and mentioned how one member of the occupying forces had been seen heading in that direction a few minutes before.

This really was the last straw, Matron reflected bitterly. Nothing ready for the boys' tea, and strangers flocking in and out of the domestic quarters like spectators at an exhibition! Goodness knows what would happen if the intruder was allowed to wander about unchecked.

As Matron hurried away to cope with this new crisis, Mr Wilkins braced himself for action.

"Come along, Carter, it's time we took a firm line," he decided, steering his colleague along the corridor in the wake of the jumble-seekers who had now disappeared from sight. "These people have simply no idea of school rules. Chaos and confusion wherever you look? Absolute bedlam! The law of the jungle!"

"The lure of the jumble would be nearer the truth," Mr Carter observed with a smile.

"It's no laughing matter," the master on duty said indignantly. "*Somebody* must have told Mrs Hackett she could bring these people here and I mean to find out who it was. And when I *do*," he went on in ominous tones, "when I *do*, I shall have something to say to whoever was responsible, you mark my words."

"Yes, of course," Mr Carter agreed soothingly. "But first of all, let's get the situation under control, shall we!"

Chapter 13

It's an Ill Wind . . .

Jennings and his helpers were unaware of the tumult raging in other parts of the building. At three o'clock they had opened the doors and admitted the queue of boys waiting outside the gymnasium for the sale to begin.

For the first twenty minutes everything went smoothly: thirty or more boys from the middle and lower forms made their way round the merchandise spread out upon the floor, laying claim to long-lost possessions and choosing free gifts of doubtful value to take home to their long-suffering families.

Binns found his string of conkers, missing since the first day of term, and chose a perished rubber hot-water bottle as a Christmas present for his aunt. Blotwell, another satisfied customer, recognised a model aircraft which he thought had been lost for ever, and selected a five-year-old calendar for an elderly uncle. He justified his choice on the grounds that his aged relative was even more out of date than the calendar.

From all sides of the room arose the steady buzz

of boys minding their own business . . . Then came the disturbance.

The first hint that all was not well was foreshadowed by the arrival of Bromwich. He came rushing up to Jennings and said, "Hey, watch it! There's a village outing heading this way at twenty-three knots. All those women on the playground."

Jennings looked at him in surprise. "Coming to the sale, d'you mean? But that's crazy. We haven't invited them."

Bromwich shrugged. "Just thought I'd warn you. If you take my advice, you'll barricade the . . . "

He broke off as the door swung open to reveal the new customers already on the threshold. "Wow! I'm going to take cover till the coast's clear," he exclaimed. "I've had a basinful of this lot already!"

At the head of the column marched Mrs Hackett enjoying her role of unofficial guide to Linbury Court. "Here we are then! This is the gymnasium," she announced. "We call it gym for short."

"Fancy that now," exclaimed Mrs Pinmill, trotting along beside her. "Just like my brother: only his Jim is short for James."

For a moment the invaders paused in the doorway gazing about them like tourists in a museum. Then Mrs Clough flourished her shopping bag as though encouraging a regiment into battle. "Come on, girls! Won't be nothing left if we don't look sharp!"

Jennings stood watching helpless and aghast as the newcomers swarmed in through the double doors and swooped down on the remains of the stock. In a matter of seconds all was confusion. Boys searching for lost property found themselves swept aside or sandwiched between rival bargain-hunters elbowing their way to the front and churning up the articles on display in their search for something worth buying.

But there *wasn't* anything worth buying! Wherever the ladies of Linbury looked, their eyes fell only upon the unwanted junk that they had rejected at the parish hall rummage sale more than a fortnight before.

A quick tour of the gymnasium was enough to convince them that they had come all the way up from the village on a fool's errand. They felt cheated, betrayed, bitterly disappointed! *This* was no way to run a jumble sale! Snorts of indignation and exclamations of protest arose from all sides of the room.

Above the hubbub, Mrs Clough's husky voice could be heard criticising the quality of the goods in the millinery department. "Disgraceful! Waste of an afternoon coming here. Connie Hackett needs her brains testing, bringing us all this way for nothing. I've a good mind to complain."

"That's right, Bertha, you do!" Mrs Pinmill encouraged her. She looked round for someone to complain to, and caught sight of Mr Wilkins making a harassed entry into the gymnasium, followed by Mr Carter looking cool and calm in the midst of the tumult going on around him.

"There you are, Bertha. Here's those two men we saw in the passage. You give them a piece of your mind."

Mrs Clough's lips set in a straight line. "I certainly will," she said.

Conditions in the overcrowded gymnasium had now

reached a state of pandemonium and Mr Wilkins had to shout to make himself heard.

"Ladies! Ladies! May I have your attention. Will you please be quiet!" he boomed with the full force of his lungs.

Gradually, the noise abated. When it had dropped to a mere ninety decibels, Mr Wilkins tried again. "I'm sorry, ladies, but there seems to have been a misunderstanding. I must ask you all to leave."

Mrs Clough spoke up firmly for the opposition. "What d'you mean, *leave*? We've only just got here."

"No doubt! But this is a private function, you see, and you have no right to be here," Mr Wilkins explained. "Technically, I'm afraid, you're all trespassing."

"*Trespassing*!" Mrs Clough's voice was shrill with anger. She elbowed her way through the crowd and waved her umbrella in Mr Wilkins' face. "Now look here, Mr Whoever-you-are, we've been messed about enough already."

The umbrella was uncomfortably close and Mr Wilkins took a step backwards as she went on, "So don't you go calling us trespassers. We've got as much right to be here as you have. We were asked to come, weren't we!"

"Asked to come?" Mr Wilkins was at a loss. "By whom?"

"You ask Connie Hackett. She'll tell you. She saw the poster."

"That's right," Mrs Hackett confirmed from the depths of the crowd. "Grand Jumble Sale, it said. Everybody Invited."

"Now look here, Mr Whoever-you-are, we've been messed about enough already".

"I don't understand. I know nothing about a . . . " Mr Wilkins broke off at the recollection of a gaudy notice in every colour of the rainbow that he had seen hanging up in the hall the day before.

He hadn't bothered to read it, beyond noting that it was some nonsense to do with Jennings' jumble sale. He glanced round and spotted the author of the poster in the middle of the crowd trying to conceal himself behind a large woman in tartan trousers.

Mr Wilkins beckoned. "Come here, Jennings!"

Deflated in spirit, the culprit made his way to the front. The invasion of the village ladies had surprised him as much as it had surprised Mr Wilkins. What was worse, it had completely ruined the function he had been at such pains to organise.

"Yes, sir?" he said, uncertainly.

"Did you invite all these people to come here this afternoon?"

Jennings hesitated. "Well, yes and no, sir. I did put some posters up, but they were just to tell the other boys about it. They weren't meant for outside people at all. I never thought anyone else would even see them, sir."

Mr Wilkins tut-tutted with exasperation. "*Doh!* You silly little boy! Don't you see what you've done! It really is too bad . . . "

He would have said more, but Mr Carter whispered in his ear that this was not a good time to hold an inquiry into Jennings' behaviour. The important thing at the moment was to restore order out of the chaos, which the boy had inadvertently caused.

With an effort Mr Wilkins restrained his feelings.

"All right then, Carter. *You* try telling these people to go home. Perhaps they'll listen to you."

Fortunately they *did* listen. Mr Carter's tactful manner eased the ruffled feelings of Mrs Clough and her friends, and by the time he had ironed out the misunderstanding, the visitors, though still resentful, were in a slightly more tolerant frame of mind.

"Might as well go home then," Mrs Clough observed with a sniff of disapproval. "Proper lot of Charleys we've been made to look. Wish now we'd never come."

"Oh, I wouldn't say that. It's been a nice change seeing round the place and all," said Mrs Pinmill. She turned inquiringly to Mr Wilkins. "Not serving teas by any chance, are you? We get it thirty pence a cup at most jumbles. Ten pence extra for biscuits."

Mr Wilkins winced and drew in his breath sharply. "No, madam, we are *not* serving teas," he said emphatically. He hoped they would hurry up and go, and held the door wide open to speed their departure.

Even so, it was a full forty minutes later before the last visitor had taken her leave, for in addition to those in the gymnasium there were others scattered about the building who had to be found and escorted off the premises.

There were Mrs Clutterbuck and her friends enjoying their picnic in the library; some of the party were still going round on their sightseeing tour; others were found taking a quiet nap in the changing-room; while upstairs in the games room the more agile members of the group were playing ping-pong.

When finally they had all been rounded up and

the evacuation was complete, Mr Wilkins' patience was worn to shreds. He closed the front door behind the last of the visitors with a sigh of relief.

He'd had a very trying afternoon, he reminded himself. And who was responsible? Jennings, of course! . . . The master-on-duty made his way back to the gymnasium, intent on having a few serious words with the organisers of the day's disasters.

He found them waiting outside in the corridor.

"Sir, please, sir, we're very sorry about what happened," Jennings greeted him, hoping to blunt the edge of his wrath with a well-timed apology.

"Sorry! So I should think," snapped Mr Wilkins. "It's entirely due to your crass stupidity that the routine of the school has been upset in this deplorable manner."

"Oh, but, sir, we never meant . . . "

"Never mind what you meant. It's what happened that I'm concerned about. Never in all my life have I had such an embarrassing situation to deal with, and I intend to punish the pair of you very severely indeed."

The culprits shifted uncomfortably from foot to foot and said nothing.

"First of all, you'll clear all that rubbish out of the gym and stack it in the kitchen yard for the dustman," Mr Wilkins went on. "When you've finished, you'll come and report to me in the staff room and I shall decide what your punishment is going to be."

"Yes, sir."

Low in spirit, the joint-managers returned to their

emporium to wind up their business affairs, while Mr Wilkins went off to the staff-room, hoping to snatch a few minutes' rest in a comfortable armchair.

Upon arriving, he found Matron and Mr Carter drinking tea together and looking unusually cheerful.

"Wonderful news, Mr Wilkins!" Matron called out as he entered. "What do you think! We've got a new cook."

"Really!" For the past hour Mr Wilkins had been so preoccupied with his own worries that he had not given another thought to Matron's concern about the catering. Now, he listened with interest as she reminded him how she had been obliged to hurry off in pursuit of the woman whom the masters had seen heading in the direction of the kitchen.

"It was lucky I did too," she went on. "She turned out to be a very experienced cook who's staying with her cousin in the village while she looks round for a job. I asked her if she'd like to work here and she accepted on the spot. In fact, she's busy at the moment cooking a hot meal for the boys' tea."

Mr Carter looked up from his tea cup. "So the advertisement in the local paper was worth while after all!"

"Oh, no! She didn't come because of that. She didn't even know about it," Matron explained. "She came because of the jumble sale."

A disgruntled snort broke from the duty master's lips. "Don't talk to me about jumble sales! That boy Jennings – and Darbishire too – are going to find themselves in very serious trouble over that. I intend to punish the pair of them in a way they won't forget."

Matron looked at him in concern. "Oh, but you *can't*, Mr Wilkins! It's entirely due to their jumble sale that we've found someone to take charge of the catering."

"Yes, I dare say but . . . "

"Now for staff supper tonight we're going to start off with onion soup followed by roast chicken with bread sauce and three sorts of vegetables, and after that . . . " Matron broke off, aware that Mr Wilkins was looking at her with the rapt expression of a starving Alpine traveller welcoming a St Bernard dog.

"What was that? *Roast chicken*, did you say?" he echoed.

"Yes, thanks to Jennings' jumble sale. If it wasn't for that, we'd still be managing on sardines and beetroot."

There was a short silence. Then Mr Wilkins said, "H'm! I see your point, Matron. Perhaps this afternoon's invasion was worth it after all." He beamed contentedly. "Roast chicken, eh! Well, well! I can't think of anything I'd like better."

Half an hour later, when Mr Wilkins was alone in the staff-room with his dreams of roast chicken, a gentle knock sounded on the door.

On the threshold stood Jennings and Darbishire looking the picture of woe. They had finished tidying the gymnasium, and all that now remained of their jumble sale was a sorry-looking mound of rubbish beside the dustbins in the kitchen yard. The horse-collar, green with mildew, lay on top of the pile like a funeral wreath mourning their ill-fated efforts.

"Please, sir, you told us to report to you." Jennings'

tone was subdued almost to a whisper. "We're terribly sorry about what happened and we promise to behave better in future." He and Darbishire had composed the speech on the way to the staff-room and rehearsed it outside the door. "We – er – we know it was our fault and we won't let it happen again, honestly, sir."

He glanced up expecting to meet a look of stern-faced disapproval. But Mr Wilkins, mellowed by the prospect of roast chicken, beamed down indulgently at the benefactors whose misguided efforts had helped to make the feast possible.

"H'm. Yes, I see what you mean," he said in kindly tones. "Of course, I've no objection to jumble sales in the ordinary way. In some cases, such as the one you organised this afternoon, the results can be well worth while."

Jennings and Darbishire stared at him in bewilderment. Was Mr Wilkins all right in his mind? Had the strain of coping with the villagers' invasion caused a mental breakdown?

"But – but I don't understand, sir," Jennings stammered. "Aren't you going to punish us for – for what we did?"

"I don't think so, Jennings. I think we'll forget the punishment this time and say no more about it."

Smiling, he closed the door on his visitors leaving them gaping at each other in puzzled wonder.

"Well, what do you know!" Jennings murmured, shaking his head in a dazed fashion. "Did you ever hear anything like it?"

"I reckon Sir must have gone stark, raving bonkers," Darbishire decided. "First, he tells us we've committed the worst crime in history, and then he turns round and says what a good idea it was!"

"That's just like masters," Jennings said knowingly. "You take it from me, Darbi, when you're grown-up you can get away with *anything*."

The unexpected reprieve left them with half an hour before tea, so they decided to devote the time to an extra rehearsal of their conjuring trick. Only three days remained before the end-of-term concert, and they were determined to give a first-class performance.

On the way down to the tuck-box room they met Venables wearing a broad smile of anticipation.

"Hey, what d'you think! Super news bulletin," he crowed. "It's sausage and mash and fried tomatoes for tea, followed by pancakes. Matron's just told me. Fabulous, isn't it! First proper meal since Mrs Cherry left." He hurried away to spread the good tidings in the common-room.

Jennings and Darbishire celebrated the feast to come with an ungainly ballet round the basement.

Then Jennings said, "That makes three important things that have all happened this afternoon." He ticked them off on his fingers. "First, our jumble sale, then Sir going off his rocker and letting us off, and now bangers for tea."

"Yes, I know. Funny how everything seems to happen at once for no reason at all, isn't it," Darbishire replied. "What you call a coincidence."

They hurried off to practise their trick, quite unaware that the three events were in any way connected.

Chapter 14

Tricky Predicament

Old boys of Linbury Court will already have received their copies of the school magazine for the Christmas term containing an account of the end-of-term concert.

From this they will have learned how the standard of singing had improved during the year, and how much the choir owed to the unsparing efforts of Mr Hind. They will have read how the Form One Percussion Band performed with verve and aplomb under the baton of R. G. Blotwell (conductor) ably supported by N. Binns (leader of the orchestra and first triangle). An appreciation of Rumbelow and Atkinson's rendering of "The Fairies' Lullaby" speaks of the performers' intense feeling and subtle variation of pace – a polite way of describing the groping for the right notes, and the five-second pauses which ensued while the piano was waiting for the violin to catch up.

Other items are also mentioned in the review. For example: *The finale which brought the house down and was received with loud applause was a hilarious skit, brilliantly acted by Jennings and Darbishire, of a would-be conjuror and his bungling assistant performing a trick that persists in going wrong.*

It is clear from this that the reporter was not in possession of the full facts, and a word of explanation is called for to show how this item could fairly be described both as a disaster and as a triumph, in one and the same breath.

Half an hour before the concert was due to begin, Mr Carter was chatting to Mr Wilkins in the staff-room.

"By the way, I gather you're going to be asked to lend your watch for a conjuring trick this evening," the senior master remarked.

"Oh, am I! Well, that's where they're going to be unlucky," Mr Wilkins said firmly. "I'm not going to have any silly little boys playing about with *my* watch. What do they want it for, anyway?"

"They want to give it a good shaking-up in a toffee tin."

"Eh! Well, of all the . . . "

"It does seem rather rough treatment. I suppose you haven't got an old one you could lend them instead?"

Mr Wilkins thought for a moment and said, "I've got a battered old thing that doesn't go. They can borrow that if they like – it's no use to me. I'll look it out before the concert starts."

Thus it was that Mr Wilkins was prompt on his cue when, during the final item, Jennings made his appeal to the audience for the loan of a valuable timepiece.

"Thank you, sir. I'll be terribly careful with it," the conjuror said in mock-solemn tones as he put the watch into an envelope and sealed down the flap. He returned to the stage where his assistant was standing ready with a toffee tin in one hand and a table-napkin in the other.

They had now reached a critical stage in the illusion. Under cover of some mirth-provoking patter, the conjuror had to shake a duplicate envelope containing a metal bottle top down his sleeve while transferring the first envelope into his assistant's pocket.

During rehearsals this part of the illusion had worked with fair success; but now that the moment of truth had arrived, the concealed envelope stuck fast in the conjuror's sleeve, and his stream of patter was punctuated by wild swinging of the arm and wriggling of the shoulder, until he seemed to be giving a display of physical education rather than sleight of hand.

Darbishire was aghast at this turn of events, but the audience were delighted and roared their approval. This was by far the most entertaining item of the evening, they decided.

For some seconds the action on the stage was confused: Jennings turned his back to the audience while Darbishire, desperate to divert their attention, danced an Irish jig in the middle of the stage.

Fortunately, the audience were too helpless with mirth to concentrate on the finer points of the deception, and eventually the conjuror's sleeve released its booty: one envelope was smuggled into Darbishire's pocket while Jennings held the other aloft for public inspection.

"And now, Matron and Gentlemen, I will place this envelope containing Mr Wilkins' valuable and priceless antique watch into this tin box," the conjuror announced, suiting the action to the word.

Then came the rattling, as noisy as pebbles in a petrol can, while the audience turned their mirth-streaming eyes on Mr Wilkins to see how he was reacting to this monstrous maltreatment of his property.

Mr Wilkins played up admirably. He shuddered and groaned in mock agony and clapped his hand over his eyes to blot out the horror of the violation.

At last the conjuror deigned to have mercy on his victim. He stopped the rattling and said, "Aha! I can see you're very worried, thinking this isn't doing your valuable watch any good, aren't you, sir?"

"Oh, yes! Very worried," the victim agreed solemnly.

"Good! Then I will now proceed to Part Two of this baffling trick. I wave my wand over the tin like so, saying the mysterious magic words, '*Oojah! Oojah! Oojah*!'"

This done, the conjuror beamed a confident smile in Mr Wilkins' direction. "Now if you will be so kind as to come up on the stage, sir, you will find that – lo and behold – your watch has mysteriously flown out of the tin into Darbishire's pocket."

The next part of the trick did not work out as described in *The Bumper Book of Indoor Hobbies*.

Mr Wilkins made his way on to the stage and removed the slight bulge which had been distorting the assistant's pocket for the past five minutes.

"Now, sir . . . " There was no disguising the note of triumph in the conjuror's voice. "Now, sir, will you kindly tell the audience what you have found."

"Certainly," said Mr Wilkins, tearing open the

container and extracting the contents. "Inside this envelope there is a metal bottle top."

"What! Oh, my goodness!" Jennings went weak at the knees and the stage swam before his eyes. How on earth had he come to mix up the envelopes and put the wrong one in Darbishire's pocket! This was disaster! This was the end of everything!

In spite of his brusque manner, Mr Wilkins was a kind man at heart and was moved by the sight of a boy in distress. Things had gone far enough, he decided; so in order to spare the conjuror's feelings and cut short the hilarity of the audience, he opened the toffee tin and retrieved his watch which had burst through its envelope during its recent rough handling. He was about to slip it unobtrusively into his pocket when, to his surprise, he noticed that the second-hand was moving. He held it up to his ear: the watch was ticking . . . !

It was entirely due to Mr Wilkins that the conjuring item was hailed as a great success. For at this point he might well have returned to his seat, reflecting that all the watch had needed to set it going was a good shaking-up. Instead, he decided to turn the laughter to good-humoured applause and restore the woebegone conjuror's shattered reputation.

He signalled to the audience to be quiet, and when the laughter had died away he made a little speech.

"Ladies and Gentlemen! We have been privileged this evening to witness a truly remarkable demonstration of magic. This watch—" He held it aloft for their inspection. "This valuable watch stopped at twenty minutes past seven one morning four years ago, and has since defied the efforts of skilled watch-repairers to make it go again. Now, charmed by the magic formula *Oojah, Oojah*, it is ticking as well as – if not better than – it ever did before."

He turned towards the conjuror fidgeting self-consciously on the other side of the stage. "I congratulate you, Mr Magician, on performing a most amazing feat. I don't know how you *intended* the trick to work, but you couldn't have provided a more sensational climax however hard you'd tried."

"Thank you, sir. I'm glad you liked it," the conjuror replied modestly.

There was a burst of applause from the audience: the curtains closed: the concert was over . . . And the term was over too, for in the morning boys and masters would all be going their different ways to enjoy their Christmas holidays.

Mr Wilkins and Mr Carter strolled back from the gymnasium together. When they reached the staff-room they found Jennings and Darbishire waiting for them outside the door.

"Sir, please sir, I just wanted to say thank you for saying what you did at the concert, sir," Jennings said. "I don't know *how* I would have finished the trick if you hadn't come to my rescue."

"That's all right," Mr Wilkins replied shortly. "No need to make a speech about it."

"And in case we don't see you in the morning, we hope you both have a really fantastic holiday," said Darbishire, beaming up at the masters through ink-spotted spectacles.

"That's very kind of you," Mr Carter replied as the dormitory bell sounded. "Goodbye, Jennings . . . Goodbye, Darbishire. And a happy Christmas."

"Thank you, sir. Same to you, sir." Jennings seized his friend from behind by both elbows and propelled him along the polished floorboards like a brake-man starting off on a blob-sleigh run. When the bob-sleigh reached the corner Jennings called back over his shoulder. "See you next term, sir! See you next term!"

Mr Wilkins winced and uttered a moan of despair. "See you next term, sir!" he mimicked. "At least he might have spared us that!"

Mr Carter smiled encouragingly. "Oh, surely, Wilkins! It's never as bad as you think."

"Don't you believe it! If you ask me, it's always a jolly sight *worse* than you think," his colleague retorted with some heat. "Just cast your mind back over the more hair-raising events of the term. Who was responsible for them?"

"Jennings, of course," Mr Carter admitted.

"Exactly! And now the silly little boy goes off for his holidays saying 'See you next term' as though it was something to look *forward* to!"

Mr Wilkins shook his head in puzzled wonder as he led the way into the staff-room. Boys were extraordinary creatures! The antics they got up to just didn't make sense to his way of thinking. He looked round and saw that Mr Carter was smiling broadly at his inability to understand the workings of the eleven-year-old mind.

For a moment Mr Wilkins felt aggrieved. Then

he, too, began to smile and a moment later he broke into a laugh that rattled the staff-room windows.

Perhaps Carter was right, he decided . . . Perhaps there *was* a funny side to it after all!